At the last turn of the corridor she halted; then very slowly took the last step, and looked, and saw.

—Saw what she had never seen, not though she had lived a hundred lives: the great vaulted cavern beneath the Tombstones, not hollowed by man's hand but by the powers of the Earth. It was jeweled with crystals and ornamented with pinnacles and filigrees of white limestone where the waters under earth had worked, eons since: immense, with glittering roof and walls, sparkling, delicate, intricate, a palace of diamonds, a house of amethyst and crystal, from which the ancient darkness had been driven out by glory.

Not bright, but dazzling to the dark-accustomed eye, was the light that worked this wonder. It was a soft gleam, like marshlight, that moved slowly across the cavern, striking a thousand scintillations from the jeweled roof and shifting a thousand fantastic shadows along the cavern walls.

The light burned at the end of a staff of wood, smokeless, unconsuming. The staff was held by a human hand. She saw the face beside the light; the dark face: the face of a man.

"Among the looms of fantasy fiction Ursula Le Guin weaves on where J. R. R. Tolkien cast off. It's a large claim; heresy perhaps to legions of Hobbit fanciers. But in a superb trilogy of novels, Le Guin's invented world of Earthsea—fuming with dragons and busy with magic—has replaced Tolkien's Middle Earth as the chosen land for high, otherworldly adventure."
—*London Sunday Times*

Bantam Books by Ursula K. Le Guin
Ask your bookseller for the books you have missed

THE BEGINNING PLACE
THE EYE OF THE HERON
VERY FAR AWAY FROM ANYWHERE ELSE

The Earthsea Trilogy

A WIZARD OF EARTHSEA
THE TOMBS OF ATUAN
THE FARTHEST SHORE

THE TOMBS
OF ATUAN

by
URSULA K. LE GUIN

Illustrated by
Gail Garraty

BANTAM BOOKS
TORONTO • NEW YORK • LONDON • SYDNEY • AUCKLAND

*This low-priced Bantam Book
has been completely reset in a type face
designed for easy reading, and was printed
from new plates. It contains the complete
text of the original hard-cover edition.*
NOT ONE WORD HAS BEEN OMITTED.

RL 6, IL 12 and up

THE TOMBS OF ATUAN

*A Bantam Spectra Book / published by arrangement with
Atheneum Publishers*

PRINTING HISTORY

Atheneum edition published September 1971
2nd printing .. February 1972   3rd printing .... March 1973
4th printing ... March 1974
A shorter version of THE TOMBS OF ATUAN *appeared in
the magazine* WORLDS OF FANTASY, *Winter, 1970-71
published by UPD Publishing Corporation.*
*Bantam edition / September 1975
19 printings through December 1985*

*Bantam Books are published by Bantam Books, Inc. Its trade-
mark, consisting of the words "Bantam Books" and the por-
trayal of a rooster, is Registered in U.S. Patent and Trademark
Office and in other countries. Marca Registrada. Bantam
Books, Inc., 666 Fifth Avenue, New York, New York 10103.*

PRINTED IN THE UNITED STATES OF AMERICA

H   28 27 26 25 24 23 22 21 20 19

For the redhead from Telluride

Contents

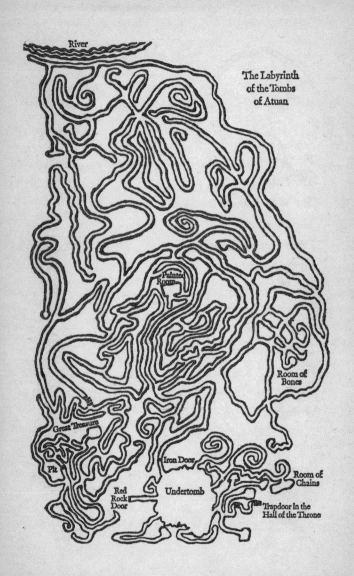

River

The Labyrinth
of the Tombs
of Atuan

Painted
Room

Room of
Bones

Great Treasure

Pit

Iron Door

Red
Rock
Door

Undertomb

Room of
Chains

Trapdoor in the
Hall of the Throne

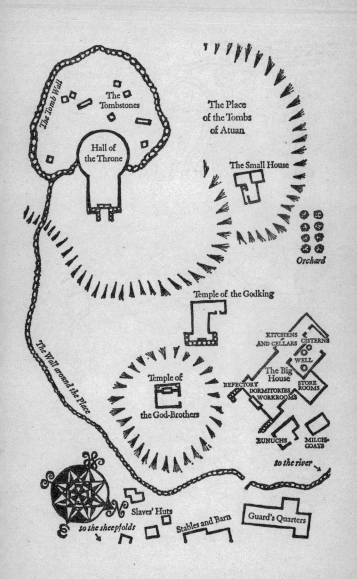

The Toms Wall

The Tombstones

Hall of the Throne

The Place of the Tombs of Atuan

The Small House

Orchard

The Wall around the Place

Temple of the Godking

KITCHENS AND CELLARS

CISTERNS

WELL

The Big House

Temple of the God-Brothers

REFECTORY

STORE ROOMS

DORMITORIES WORKROOMS

EUNUCHS

MILCH-GOATS

to the river

Slaves' Huts

to the sheepfolds

Stables and Barn

Guard's Quarters

Prologue

"Come home, Tenar! Come home!"

In the deep valley, in the twilight, the apple trees were on the eve of blossoming; here and there among the shadowed boughs one flower had opened early, rose and white, like a faint star. Down the orchard aisles, in the thick, new, wet grass, the little girl ran for the joy of running; hearing the call she did not come at once, but made a long circle before she turned her face towards home. The mother waiting in the doorway of the hut, with the firelight behind her, watched the tiny figure running and bobbing like a bit of thistledown blown over the darkening grass beneath the trees.

1

By the corner of the hut, scraping clean an earth-clotted hoe, the father said, "Why do you let your heart hang on the child? They're coming to take her away next month. For good. Might as well bury her and be done with it. What's the good of clinging to one you're bound to lose? She's no good to us. If they'd pay for her when they took her, that would be something, but they won't. They'll take her and that's an end of it."

The mother said nothing, watching the child who had stopped to look up through the trees. Over the high hills, above the orchards, the evening star shone piercing clear.

"She isn't ours, she never was since they came here and said she must be the Priestess at the Tombs. Why can't you see that?" The man's voice was harsh with complaint and bitterness. "You have four others. They'll stay here, and this one won't. So, don't set your heart on her. Let her go!"

"When the time comes," the woman said, "I will let her go." She bent to meet the child who came running on little, bare, white feet across the muddy ground, and gathered her up in her arms. As she turned to enter the hut she bent her head to kiss the child's hair, which was black; but her own hair, in the flicker of firelight from the hearth, was fair.

The man stood outside, his own feet bare and cold on the ground, the clear sky of spring darkening above him. His face in the dusk was full of grief, a dull, heavy, angry grief that he would never find the words to say. At last he shrugged, and followed his wife into the firelit room that rang with children's voices.

The Eaten One

One high horn shrilled and ceased. The silence that followed was shaken only by the sound of many footsteps keeping time with a drum struck softly at a slow heartpace. Through cracks in the roof of the Hall of the Throne, gaps between columns where a whole section of masonry and tile had collapsed, unsteady sunlight shone aslant. It was an hour after sunrise. The air was still and cold. Dead leaves of weeds that had forced up between marble pavement-tiles were outlined with frost, and crackled, catching on the long black robes of the priestesses.

They came, four by four, down the vast hall between double rows of columns. The drum beat dully. No voice spoke, no eye watched. Torches carried by black-clad girls burned reddish in the shafts of sunlight, brighter in the dusk between. Outside, on the steps of the Hall of the Throne, the men stood, guards, trumpeters, drummers; within the great doors only women had come, dark-robed and hooded, walking slowly four by four towards the empty throne.

Two came, tall women looming in their black, one of them thin and rigid, the other heavy, swaying with the planting of her feet. Between these two walked a child of about six. She wore a straight white shift. Her head and arms and legs were bare, and she was barefoot. She looked extremely small. At the foot of the steps leading up to the throne, where the others now waited in dark rows, the two tall women halted. They pushed the child forward a little.

The throne on its high platform seemed to be curtained on each side with great webs of blackness dropping from the gloom of the roof; whether these were curtains, or only denser shadows, the eye could not make certain. The throne itself was black, with a dull glimmer of precious stones or gold on the arms and back, and it was huge. A man sitting in it would have been dwarfed; it was not of human dimensions. It was empty. Nothing sat in it but shadows.

Alone, the child climbed up four of the seven steps of red-veined marble. They were so broad and high that she had to get both feet onto one step before attempting the next. On the middle step, directly in front of the throne, stood a large, rough block of wood, hollowed out on top. The child knelt on both knees and fitted her head into the hollow, turning it a little sideways. She knelt there without moving.

A figure in a belted gown of white wool stepped suddenly out of the shadows at the right of the throne and strode down the steps to the child. His face was masked with white. He held a sword of polished steel five feet long. Without word or hesitation he swung the sword, held in both hands, up over the little girl's neck. The drum stopped beating.

As the blade swung to its highest point and poised, a figure in black darted out from the left side of the throne, leapt down the stairs, and stayed the sacrificer's arms with slenderer arms. The sharp edge of the sword glittered in mid-air. So they balanced for a moment, the white figure and the black, both faceless, dancer-like above the motionless child whose white neck was bared by the parting of her black hair.

In silence each leapt aside and up the stairs again, vanishing in the darkness behind the enormous throne. A priestess came forward and poured out a bowl of some liquid on the steps beside the kneeling child. The stain looked black in the dimness of the hall.

The child got up and descended the four stairs laboriously. When she stood at the bottom, the two tall priestesses put on her a black robe and hood and mantle, and turned her around again to face the steps, the dark stain, the throne.

"O let the Nameless Ones behold the girl given to them, who is verily the one born ever nameless. Let them accept her life and the years of her life until her death, which is also theirs. Let them find her acceptable. Let her be eaten!"

Other voices, shrill and harsh as trumpets, replied: "She is eaten! She is eaten!"

The little girl stood looking from under her black cowl up at the throne. The jewels inset in the huge clawed arms and the back were glazed with dust, and on the carven back were cobwebs and whitish stains of owl droppings. The three highest steps directly before the throne, above the step on which she had knelt, had never been climbed by mortal feet. They were so thick with dust that they looked like one slant of gray soil, the planes of the red-veined marble wholly hidden by the unstirred, untrodden siftings of how many years, how many centuries.

"She is eaten! She is eaten!"

Now the drum, abrupt, began to sound again, beating a quicker pace.

Silent and shuffling, the procession formed and moved away from the throne, eastward towards the bright, distant square of the doorway. On either side, the thick double columns, like the calves of immense pale legs, went up to the dusk under the ceiling. Among the priestesses, and now all in black like them, the child walked, her small bare feet treading solemnly over the frozen weeds, the icy stones. When sunlight slanting through the ruined roof flashed across her way, she did not look up.

Guards held the great doors wide. The black procession came out into the thin, cold light and wind of early morning. The sun dazzled, swimming above the eastern vastness. Westward, the mountains caught its yellow light, as did the facade of the Hall of the Throne. The other buildings, lower on the hill, still lay in purplish shadow, except for the Temple of the God-Brothers across the way on a little knoll: its roof, newly gilt, flashed the day back in glory. The black line of priestesses, four by four, wound down the Hill of the Tombs, and as they went they began softly to chant. The tune was on three notes only, and the word that was repeated over and over was a word so old it had lost its meaning, like a signpost still standing when the road is gone. Over and over they chanted the empty word. All that day of the Remaking of the Priestess was filled with the low chanting of women's voices, a dry unceasing drone.

The little girl was taken from room to room, from temple to temple. In one place salt was placed upon her tongue; in another she knelt facing west while her hair was cut short and washed with oil and scented vinegar; in another she lay face down on a slab of black marble behind an altar while shrill voices sang a lament for the dead. Neither she nor any of the priestesses ate food or drank water all that day. As the evening star set, the little girl was put to bed, naked between sheepskin rugs, in a room she had never slept in before. It was in a house that had been locked for years, unlocked only that day. The room was higher than it was long, and had no windows. There was a dead smell in it, still and stale. The silent women left her there in the dark.

She held still, lying just as they had put her. Her eyes were wide open. She lay so for a long time.

She saw light shake on the high wall. Someone came

quietly along the corridor, shielding a rushlight so it showed no more light than a firefly. A husky whisper: "Ho, are you there, Tenar?"

The child did not reply.

A head poked in the doorway, a strange head, hairless as a peeled potato, and of the same yellowish color. The eyes were like potato-eyes, brown and tiny. The nose was dwarfed by great, flat slabs of cheek, and the mouth was a lipless slit. The child stared unmoving at this face. Her eyes were large, dark, and fixed.

"Ho, Tenar, my little honeycomb, there you are!" The voice was husky, high as a woman's voice but not a woman's voice. "I shouldn't be here, I belong outside the door, on the porch, that's where I go. But I had to see how my little Tenar is, after all the long day of it, eh, how's my poor little honeycomb?"

He moved towards her, noiseless and burly, and put out his hand as if to smooth back her hair.

"I am not Tenar any more," the child said, staring up at him. His hand stopped; he did not touch her.

"No," he said, after a moment, whispering. "I know. I know. Now you're the little Eaten One. But I . . ."

She said nothing.

"It was a hard day for a little one," the man said, shuffling, the tiny light flickering in his big yellow hand.

"You should not be in this House, Manan."

"No. No. I know. I shouldn't be in this House. Well, good night, little one. . . . Good night."

The child said nothing. Manan slowly turned around and went away. The glimmer died from the high cell walls. The little girl, who had no name any more but *Arha*, the Eaten One, lay on her back looking steadily at the dark.

The Wall
Around the Place

As she grew older she lost all remembrance of her mother, without knowing she had lost it. She belonged here, at the Place of the Tombs; she had always belonged here. Only sometimes in the long evenings of July as she watched the western mountains, dry and lion-colored in the afterglow of sunset, she would think of a fire that had burned on a hearth, long ago, with the same clear yellow light. And with this came a memory of being held, which was strange, for here she was seldom even touched; and the memory of a pleasant smell, the fragrance of hair freshly washed and rinsed in sage-scented water, fair long hair, the color of sunset and firelight. That was all she had left.

She knew more than she remembered, of course, for

she had been told the whole story. When she was seven or eight years old, and first beginning to wonder who indeed this person called "Arha" was, she had gone to her guardian, the Warden Manan, and said, "Tell me how I was chosen, Manan."

"Oh, you know all that, little one."

And indeed she did; the tall, dry-voiced priestess Thar had told her till she knew the words by heart, and she recited them: "Yes, I know. At the death of the One Priestess of the Tombs of Atuan, the ceremonies of burial and purification are completed within one month by the moon's calendar. After this certain of the Priestesses and Wardens of the Place of the Tombs go forth across the desert, among the towns and villages of Atuan, seeking and asking. They seek the girl-child who was born on the night of the Priestess' death. When they find such a child, they wait and they watch. The child must be sound of body and of mind, and as it grows it must not suffer from rickets nor the smallpox nor any deformity, nor become blind. If it reaches the age of five years unblemished, then it is known that the body of the child is indeed the new body of the Priestess who died. And the child is made known to the Godking in Awabath, and brought here to her Temple and instructed for a year. And at the year's end she is taken to the Hall of the Throne and her name is given back to those who are her Masters, the Nameless Ones: for she is the nameless one, the Priestess Ever Reborn."

This was all word for word as Thar had told her, and she had never dared ask for a word more. The thin priestess was not cruel, but she was very cold and lived by an iron law, and Arha was in awe of her. But she was not in awe of Manan, far from it, and she would command him, "Now tell me how *I* was chosen!" And he would tell her again.

"We left here, going north and west, in the third day of the moon's waxing; for Arha-that-was had died in the third day of the last moon. And first we went to Tenacbah, which is a great city, though those who've seen both say it's no more to Awabath than a flea to a cow. But it's big enough for me, there must be ten hundred houses in Tenacbah! And we went on to Gar. But nobody in those cities had a baby girl born to them on the third day of the moon a month before; there were some had boys, but boys won't do. . . . So we went into the hill country north of Gar, to the towns and villages. That's my own land. I was born in the hills there, where the rivers run, and the land is green. Not in this desert." Manan's husky voice would get a strange sound when he said that, and his small eyes would be quite hidden in their folds; he would pause a little, and at last go on. "And so we found and spoke to all those who were parents of babies born in the last months. And some would lie to us. 'Oh yes, surely our baby girl was born on the moon's third day!' For poor folk, you know, are often glad to get rid of girl-babies. And there were others who were so poor, living in lonely huts in the valleys of the hills, that they kept no count of days and scarce knew how to tell the turn of time, so they could not say for certain how old their baby was. But we could always come at the truth, by asking long enough. But it was slow work. At last we found a girl-child, in a village of ten houses, in the orchard-vales westward of Entat. Eight months old she was, so long had we been looking. But she had been born on the night that the Priestess of the Tombs had died, and within the very hour of her death. And she was a fine baby, sitting up on her mother's knee and looking with bright eyes at all of us, crowding into the one room of the house like bats into a cave! The father was a poor man. He tended the apple trees of the rich man's orchard, and had nothing of his own but five children and a goat. Not even the house was his. So there we all crowded in, and you could tell by the way the priestesses looked at the baby and spoke among themselves that they thought they had found the Reborn One at last. And the mother could tell this too. She held the baby and never said a word. Well, so, the next day we came back. And look here! The little bright-eyed baby lying in a cot of rushes weeping and screaming, and all over its body weals and red rashes of fever, and the mother wailing louder than the baby, 'Oh! Oh! My

babe hath the Witch-Fingers on her!' That's how she
said it; the smallpox she meant. In my village, too, they
called it the Witch-Fingers. But Kossil, she who is now
the High Priestess of the Godking, she went to the cot
and picked up the baby. The others had all drawn
back, and I with them; I don't value my life very high,
but who enters a house where smallpox is? But she had
no fear, not that one. She picked up the baby and said,
'It has no fever.' And she spat on her finger and rubbed
at the red marks, and they came off. They were
only berry juice. The poor silly mother had thought to
fool us and keep her child!" Manan laughed heartily at
this; his yellow face hardly changed, but his sides
heaved. "So, her husband beat her, for he was afraid of
the wrath of the priestesses. And soon we came back to
the desert, but each year one of the people of the Place
would return to the village among the apple orchards,
and see how the child got on. So five years passed, and
then Thar and Kossil made the journey, with the Temple guards, and soldiers of the red helmet sent by the
Godking to escort them safely. They brought the child
back here, for it was indeed the Priestess of the Tombs
reborn, and here it belonged. And who was the child,
eh, little one?"

"Me," said Arha, looking off into the distance as if
to see something she could not see, something gone out
of sight.

Once she asked, "What did the . . . the mother do,
when they came to take the child away?"

But Manan didn't know; he had not gone with the
priestesses on that final journey.

And she could not remember. What was the good in
remembering? It was gone, all gone. She had come
where she must come. In all the world she knew only
one place: the Place of the Tombs of Atuan.

In her first year there she had slept in the big dormitory with the other novices, girls between four and
fourteen. Even then Manan had been set apart among
the Ten Wardens as her particular guardian, and her
cot had been in a little alcove, partly separated from
the long, low-beamed main room of the dormitory in

the Big House where the girls giggled and whispered before they slept, and yawned and plaited one another's hair in the gray light of morning. When her name was taken from her and she became Arha, she slept alone in the Small House, in the bed and in the room that would be her bed and her room for the rest of her life. That house was hers, the House of the One Priestess, and no one might enter it without her permission. When she was quite little still, she enjoyed hearing people knock submissively on her door, and saying, "You may come in," and it annoyed her that the two High Priestesses, Kossil and Thar, took their permission for granted and entered her house without knocking.

The days went by, the years went by, all alike. The girls of the Place of the Tombs spent their time at classes and disciplines. They did not play any games. There was no time for games. They learned the sacred songs and the sacred dances, the histories of the Kargad Lands, and the mysteries of whichever of the gods they were dedicated to: the Godking who ruled in Awabath, or the Twin Brothers, Atwah and Wuluah. Of them all, only Arha learned the rites of the Nameless Ones, and these were taught her by one person, Thar, the High Priestess of the Twin Gods. This took her away from the others for an hour or more daily, but most of her day, like theirs, was spent simply working. They learned how to spin and weave the wool of their flocks, and how to plant and harvest and prepare the food they always ate: lentils, buckwheat ground to a coarse meal for porridge or a fine flour for unleavened bread, onions, cabbages, goat-cheese, apples, and honey.

The best thing that could happen was to be allowed to go fishing in the murky green river that flowed through the desert a half mile northeast of the Place; to take along an apple or a cold buckwheat bannock for lunch and sit all day in the dry sunlight among the reeds, watching the slow green water run and the cloud-shadows change slowly on the mountains. But if you squealed with excitement when the line tensed and you swung in a flat, glittering fish to flop on the river-bank and drown in air, then Mebbeth would hiss like an adder, "Be still, you screeching fool!" Mebbeth, who served in the Godking's temple, was a dark woman, still young, but hard and sharp as obsidian. Fishing was her passion. You had to keep on her good side, and never make a sound, or she would not take you out to fish again; and then you'd never get to the river except to fetch water in summer when the wells ran low. That was a dreary business, to trudge through the searing white heat a half mile down to the river, fill the two buckets on their carrying pole, and then set off as fast as possible uphill to the Place. The first hundred yards were easy, but then the buckets began to grow heavier, and the pole burned your shoulders like a bar of hot iron, and the light glared on the dry road, and every step was harder and slower. At last you got to the cool shade of the back courtyard of the Big House by the vegetable patch, and dumped the buckets into the great cistern with a splash. And then you had to turn around to do it all over again, and again, and again.

Within the precincts of the Place—that was all the name it had or needed, for it was the most ancient and sacred of all places in the Four Lands of the Kargish Empire—a couple of hundred people lived, and there were many buildings: three temples, the Big House and the Small House, the quarters of the eunuch wardens, and close outside the wall the guards' barracks and many slaves' huts, the storehouses and sheep pens and goat pens and farm buildings. It looked like a little town, seen from a distance, from up on the dry hills westward where nothing grew but sage, wire-grass in straggling clumps, small weeds and desert herbs. Even from away off on the eastern plains, looking up one might see the gold roof of the Temple of the Twin Gods wink and glitter beneath the mountains, like a speck of mica in a shelf of rock.

That temple itself was a cube of stone, plastered white, windowless, with a low porch and door. Showier, and centuries newer, was the Temple of the Godking a little below it, with a high portico and a row of thick white columns with painted capitals—each one a solid log of cedar, brought on shipboard from Hur-at-Hur where there are forests, and dragged by the straining of twenty slaves across the barren plains to the Place. Only after a traveler approaching from the east had seen the gold roof and the bright columns would he see, higher up on the Hill of the Place, above them all, tawny and ruinous as the desert itself, the oldest of the temples of his race: the huge, low Hall of the Throne, with patched walls and flattish, crumbling dome.

Behind the Hall and encircling the whole crest of the hill ran a massive wall of rock, laid without mortar and half fallen down in many places. Inside the loop of the wall several black stones eighteen or twenty feet high stuck up like huge fingers out of the earth. Once the eye saw them it kept returning to them. They stood there full of meaning, and yet there was no saying what they meant. There were nine of them. One stood straight, the others leaned more or less, two had fallen. They were crusted with gray and orange lichen as if splotched with paint, all but one, which was naked and black, with a dull gloss to it. It was smooth to the touch, but on the others, under the crust of lichen, vague carvings could be seen, or felt with the fingers— shapes, signs. These nine stones were the Tombs of Atuan. They had stood there, it was said, since the time of the first men, since Earthsea was created. They had been planted in the darkness when the lands were raised up from the ocean's depths. They were older by far than the Godkings of Kargad, older than the Twin Gods, older than light. They were the tombs of those who ruled before the world of men came to be, the ones not named, and she who served them had no name.

She did not go among them often, and no one else ever set foot on that ground where they stood, on the hilltop within the rock wall behind the Hall of the Throne. Twice a year, at the full moon nearest the equinox of spring and of autumn, there was a sacrifice before the Throne and she came out from the low back door of the Hall carrying a great brass basin full of smoking goat's blood; this she must pour out, half at the foot of the standing black stone, half over one of the fallen stones which lay embedded in the rocky dirt, stained by the blood-offering of centuries.

Sometimes Arha went by herself in the early morning and wandered among the Stones trying to make out the dim humps and scratches of the carvings, brought out more clearly by the low angle of the light; or she would sit there and look up at the mountains westward, and down at the roofs and walls of the Place all laid out below, and watch the first stirrings of activity around the Big House and the guards' barracks, and the flocks of sheep and goats going off to their sparse pastures by the river. There was never anything to do among the Stones. She went only because it was permitted her to go there, because there she was alone. It was a dreary place. Even in the heat of noon in the desert summer there was a coldness about it. Sometimes the wind whistled a little between the two stones that stood closest together, leaning together as if telling secrets. But no secret was told.

From the Tomb Wall another, lower rock wall ran, making a long irregular semicircle about the Hill of the Place and then trailing off northward towards the river. It did not so much protect the Place, as cut it in two: on one side the temples and houses of the priestesses and wardens, on the other the quarters of the guards and of the slaves who farmed and herded and foraged for the Place. None of these ever crossed the wall, except that on certain very holy festivals the guards, and their drummers and players of the horn, would attend the procession of the priestesses; but they did not enter the portals of the temples. No other men set foot upon the inner ground of the Place. There had once been pilgrimages, kings and chieftains coming from the Four Lands to worship there; the first Godking, a century and a half ago, had come to enact the rites of his own temple. Yet even he could not enter among the Tombstones, even he had had to eat and sleep outside the wall around the Place.

One could climb that wall easily enough, fitting toes into crevices. The Eaten One and a girl called Penthe were sitting up on the wall one afternoon in late spring.

They were both twelve years old. They were supposed to be in the weaving room of the Big House, a huge stone attic; they were supposed to be at the great looms always warped with dull black wool, weaving black cloth for robes. They had slipped outside for a drink at the well in the courtyard, and then Arha had said, "Come on!" and had led the other girl down the hill, around out of sight of the Big House, to the wall. Now they sat on top of it, ten feet up, their bare legs dangling down on the outside, looking over the flat plains that went on and on to the east and north.

"I'd like to see the sea," said Penthe.

"What for?" said Arha, chewing a bitter stem of milkweed she had picked from the wall. The barren land was just past its flowering. All the small desert blossoms, yellow and rose and white, low-growing and quick-flowering, were going to seed, scattering tiny plumes and parasols of ash white on the wind, dropping their hooked, ingenious burrs. The ground under the apple trees of the orchard was a drift of bruised white and pink. The branches were green, the only green trees within miles of the Place. Everything else, from horizon to horizon, was a dull, tawny, desert color, except that the mountains had a silvery bluish tinge from the first buds of the flowering sage.

"Oh, I don't know what for. I'd just like to see something different. It's always the same here. Nothing happens."

"All that happens everywhere, begins here," said Arha.

"Oh, I know. . . . But I'd like to see some of it happening!"

Penthe smiled. She was a soft, comfortable-looking girl. She scratched the soles of her bare feet on the sun-warmed rocks, and after a while went on, "You know, I used to live by the sea when I was little. Our village was right behind the dunes, and we used to go down and play on the beach sometimes. Once I remember we saw a fleet of ships going by, way out at sea. The ships looked like dragons with red wings. Some of them had real necks, with dragon heads. They came sailing by

Atuan, but they weren't Kargish ships. They came from the west, from the Inner Lands, the headman said. Everybody came down to watch them. I think they were afraid they might land. They just went by, nobody knew where they were going. Maybe to make war in Karego-At. But think of it, they really came from the sorcerers' islands, where all the people are the color of dirt and they can all cast a spell on you easy as winking."

"Not on me," Arha said fiercely. "I wouldn't have looked at them. They're vile accursed sorcerers. How dare they sail so close to the Holy Land?"

"Oh, well, I suppose the Godking will conquer them some day and make them all slaves. But I wish I could see the sea again. There used to be little octopuses in the tide pools, and if you shouted 'Boo!' at them they turned all white.—There comes that old Manan, looking for you."

Arha's guard and servant was coming slowly along the inner side of the wall. He would stoop to pull a wild onion, of which he held a large, limp bunch, then straighten up and look about him with his small, dull, brown eyes. He had grown fatter with the years, and his hairless yellow skin glistened in the sun.

"Slide down part way on the men's side," Arha hissed, and both girls wriggled lithe as lizards down the far side of the wall until they could cling there just below the top, invisible from the inner side. They heard Manan's slow footsteps coming by.

"Hoo! Hoo! Potato face!" crooned Arha, a whispering jeer faint as the wind among the grasses.

The heavy tread halted. "Ho there," said the uncertain voice. "Little one? Arha?"

Silence.

Manan went forward.

"Hoo-oo! Potato face!"

"Hoo, potato belly!" Penthe whispered in imitation, and then moaned, trying to suppress giggles.

"Somebody there?"

Silence.

"Oh well, well, well," the eunuch sighed, and his

slow feet went on. When he was gone over the shoulder of the slope, the girls scrambled back up onto the top of the wall. Penthe was pink with sweat and giggles, but Arha looked savage.

"The stupid old bellwether, following me around everywhere!"

"He has to," Penthe said reasonably. "It's his job, looking after you."

"Those I serve look after me. I please them; I need please nobody else. These old women and half-men, these people should leave me alone. I am the One Priestess!"

Penthe stared at the other girl. "Oh," she said feebly, "oh, I know you are, Arha—"

"Then they should let me be. And not order me about all the time!"

Penthe said nothing for a while, but sighed, and sat swinging her plump legs and gazing at the vast, pale lands below, that rose so slowly to a high, vague, immense horizon.

"You'll get to give the orders pretty soon, you know," she said at last, quietly. "In two more years we won't be children any more. We'll be fourteen. I'll go into the Godking's temple, and things will be about the same for me. But you'll really be the High Priestess then. Even Kossil and Thar will have to obey you."

The Eaten One said nothing. Her face was set, her eyes under black brows caught the light of the sky in a pale glitter.

"We ought to go back," Penthe said.

"No."

"But the weaving mistress might tell Thar. And soon it'll be time for the Nine Chants."

"I'm staying here. You stay, too."

"They won't punish you, but they will punish me," Penthe said in her mild way. Arha did not reply. Penthe sighed, and stayed. The sun was sinking into haze high above the plains. Far away on the long, gradual slant of the land, sheep bells clanked faintly and lambs bleated. The spring wind blew in dry, faint gusts, sweet-smelling.

The Nine Chants were nearly over when the two girls returned. Mebbeth had seen them sitting on the 'Men's Wall' and had reported this to her superior, Kossil, High Priestess of the Godking.

Kossil was heavy-footed, heavy-faced. Without expression in face or voice she spoke to the two girls, telling them to follow her. She led them through the stone hallways of the Big House, out the front door, up the knoll to the Temple of Atwah and Wuluah. There she spoke with the High Priestess of that temple, Thar, tall and dry and thin as the legbone of a deer.

Kossil said to Penthe, "Take off your gown."

She whipped the girl with a bundle of reed canes, which cut the skin a little. Penthe bore this patiently, with silent tears. She was sent back to the weaving room without supper, and the next day also she would go without food. "If you are found climbing over the Men's Wall again," Kossil said, "there will be very much worse things than this happen to you. Do you understand, Penthe?" Kossil's voice was soft, but not kindly. Penthe said, "Yes," and slipped away, cowering and flinching as her heavy clothing rubbed the cuts on her back.

Arha had stood beside Thar to watch the whipping. Now she watched Kossil clean the canes of the whip.

Thar said to her, "It is not fitting that you be seen climbing and running with other girls. You are Arha."

She stood sullen and did not reply.

"It is better that you do only what is needful for you to do. You are Arha."

For a moment the girl raised her eyes to Thar's face, then to Kossil's, and there was a depth of hate or rage in her look that was terrible to see. But the thin priestess showed no concern; rather she confirmed it, leaning forward a little, almost whispering, "*You are Arha.* There is nothing left. It was all eaten."

"It was all eaten," the girl repeated, as she had repeated daily, all the days of her life since she was six.

Thar bowed her head slightly; so did Kossil, as she put away the whip. The girl did not bow, but turned submissively and left.

After the supper of potatoes and spring onions, eaten in silence in the narrow, dark refectory, after the chanting of the evening hymns, and the placing of the sacred words upon the doors, and the brief Ritual of the Unspoken, the work of the day was done. Now the girls might go up to the dormitory and play games with dice and sticks, so long as the single rushlight burned, and whisper in the dark from bed to bed. Arha set off across the courts and slopes of the Place as she did every night, to the Small House where she slept alone.

The night wind was sweet. The stars of spring shone thick, like drifts of daisies in spring meadows, like the glittering of light on the April sea. But the girl had no memory of meadows or the sea. She did not look up.

"Ho there, little one!"

"Manan," she said indifferently.

The big shadow shuffled up beside her, starlight glinting on his hairless pate.

"Were you punished?"

"I can't be punished."

"No. . . . That's so. . . ."

"They can't punish me. They don't dare."

He stood with his big hands hanging, dim and bulky. She smelled wild onion, and the sweaty, sagey smell of his old black robes, which were torn at the hem, and too short for him.

"They can't touch me. I am Arha," she said in a shrill, fierce voice, and burst into tears.

The big, waiting hands came up and drew her to him, held her gently, smoothed her braided hair. "There, there. Little honeycomb, little girl. . . ." She heard the husky murmur in the deep hollow of his chest, and clung to him. Her tears stopped soon, but she held onto Manan as if she could not stand up.

"Poor little one," he whispered, and picking the child up carried her to the doorway of the house where she slept alone. He set her down.

"All right now, little one?"

She nodded, turned from him, and entered the dark house.

The Prisoners

Kossil's steps sounded along the hallway of the Small House, even and deliberate. The tall, heavy figure filled the doorway of the room, shrank as the priestess bowed down touching one knee to the floor, swelled as she straightened to her full height.

"Mistress."

"What is it, Kossil?"

"I have been permitted to look after certain matters pertaining to the Domain of the Nameless Ones, until now. If you so desire, it is now time for you to learn, and see, and take charge of these matters, which you have not yet remembered in this life."

The girl had been sitting in her windowless room, supposedly meditating, actually doing nothing and thinking almost nothing. It took some time for the

23

fixed, dull, haughty expression of her face to change. Yet it did change, though she tried to conceal it. She said, with a certain slyness, "The Labyrinth?"

"We will not enter the Labyrinth. But it will be necessary to cross the Undertomb."

There was a tone in Kossil's voice that might have been fear, or might have been a pretense of fear, intended to frighten Arha. The girl stood up without haste and said indifferently, "Very well." But in her heart, as she followed the heavy figure of the Godking's priestess, she exulted: At last! At last! I shall see my own domain at last!

She was fifteen. It was over a year since she had made her crossing into womanhood and at the same time had come into her full powers as the One Priestess of the Tombs of Atuan, highest of all high priestesses of the Kargad Lands, one whom not even the Godking himself might command. They all bowed the knee to her now, even grim Thar and Kossil. All spoke to her with elaborate deference. But nothing had changed. Nothing happened. Once the ceremonies of her consecration were over, the days went on as they had always gone. There was wool to be spun, black cloth to be woven, meal to be ground, rites to be performed; the Nine Chants must be sung nightly, the doorways blessed, the Stones fed with goat's blood twice a year, the dances of the dark of the moon danced before the Empty Throne. And so the whole year had passed, just as the years before it had passed, and were all the years of her life to pass so?

Her boredom rose so strong in her sometimes that it felt like terror: it took her by the throat. Not long ago she had been driven to speak of it. She had to talk, she thought, or she would go mad. It was Manan she talked to. Pride kept her from confiding in the other girls, and caution kept her from confession to the older women, but Manan was nothing, a faithful old bell-wether; it didn't matter what she said to him. To her surprise he had had an answer for her.

"Long ago," he said, "you know, little one, before our four lands joined together into an empire, before

there was a Godking over us all, there were a lot of
lesser kings, princes, chiefs. They were always quarreling with each other. And they'd come here to settle
their quarrels. That was how it was, they'd come from
our land Atuan, and from Karego-At, and Atnini, and
even from Hur-at-Hur, all the chiefs and princes with
their servants and their armies. And they'd ask you
what to do. And you'd go before the Empty Throne,
and give them the counsel of the Nameless Ones. Well,
that was long ago. After a while the Priest-Kings came
to rule all of Karego-At, and soon they were ruling
Atuan; and now for four or five lifetimes of men the
Godkings have ruled all the four lands together, and
made them an empire. And so things are changed. The
Godking can put down the unruly chiefs, and settle all
the quarrels himself. And being a god, you see, he
doesn't have to consult the Nameless Ones very often."

Arha stopped to think this over. Time did not mean
very much, here in the desert land, under the unchang-
ing Stones, leading a life that had been led in the same
way since the beginning of the world. She was not ac-
customed to thinking about things changing, old ways
dying and new ones arising. She did not find it comfortable to look at things in that light. "The powers of
the Godking are much less than the powers of the Ones
I serve," she said, frowning.

"Surely.... Surely.... But one doesn't go about
saying that to a god, little honeycomb. Nor to his
priestess."

And catching his small, brown, twinkling eye, she
thought of Kissil, High Priestess of the Godking, whom
she had feared ever since she first came to the Place;
and she took his meaning.

"But the Godking, and his people, are neglecting the
worship of the Tombs. No one comes."

"Well, he sends prisoners here to sacrifice. He doesn't
neglect that. Nor the gifts due to the Nameless Ones."

"Gifts! His temple is painted fresh every year, there's
a hundredweight of gold on the altar, the lamps burn
attar of roses! And look at the Hall of the Throne—
holes in the roof, and the dome cracking, and the walls

full of mice, and owls, and bats. . . . But all the same it will outlast the Godking and all his temples, and all the kings that come after him. It was there before them, and when they're all gone it will still be there. It is the center of things."

"It is the center of things."

"There are riches there; Thar tells me about them sometimes. Enough to fill the Godking's temple ten times over. Gold and trophies given ages ago, a hundred generations, who knows how long. They're all locked away in the pits and vaults, underground. They won't take me there yet, they keep me waiting and waiting. But I know what it's like. There are rooms underneath the Hall, underneath the whole Place, under where we stand now. There's a great maze of tunnels, a Labyrinth. It's like a great dark city, under the hill. Full of gold, and the swords of old heroes, and old crowns, and bones, and years, and silence."

She spoke as if in trance, in rapture. Manan watched her. His slabby face never expressed much but stolid, careful sadness; it was sadder than usual now. "Well, and you're mistress of all that," he said. "The silence, and the dark."

"I am. But they won't show me anything, only the rooms above ground, behind the Throne. They haven't even shown me the entrances to the places underground; they just mumble about them sometimes. They're keeping my own domain from me! Why do they make me wait and wait?"

"You are young. And perhaps," Manan said in his husky alto, "perhaps they're afraid, little one. It's not their domain, after all. It's yours. They are in danger when they enter there. There's no mortal that doesn't fear the Nameless Ones."

Arha said nothing, but her eyes flashed. Again Manan had shown her a new way of seeing things. So formidable, so cold, so strong had Thar and Kossil always seemed to her, that she had never even imagined their being afraid. Yet Manan was right. They feared those places, those powers of which Arha was part, to which she belonged. They were afraid to go into the dark places, lest they be eaten.

Now, as she went with Kossil down the steps of the Small House and up the steep winding path towards the Hall of the Throne, she recalled that conversation with Manan, and exulted again. No matter where they took her, what they showed her, she would not be afraid. She would know her way.

A little behind her on the path, Kossil spoke. "One of my mistress' duties, as she knows, is the sacrifice of certain prisoners, criminals of noble birth, who by sacrilege or treason have sinned against our lord the Godking."

"Or against the Nameless Ones," said Arha.

"Truly. Now it is not fitting that the Eaten One while yet a child should undertake this duty. But my mistress is no longer a child. There are prisoners in the Room of Chains, sent a month ago by the grace of our lord the Godking from his city Awabath."

"I did not know prisoners had come. Why did I not know?"

"Prisoners are brought at night, and secretly, in the way prescribed of old in the rituals of the Tombs. It is the secret way my mistress will follow, if she takes the path that leads along the wall."

Arha turned off the path to follow the great wall of stone that bounded the Tombs behind the domed hall. The rocks it was built of were massive; the least of them would outweigh a man, and the largest were big as wagons. Though unshapen they were carefully fitted and interlocked. Yet in places the height of the wall had slipped down and the rocks lay in a shapeless heap. Only a vast span of time could do that, the desert centuries of fiery days and frozen nights, the millennial, imperceptible movements of the hills themselves.

"It is very easy to climb the Tomb Wall," Arha said as they went along beneath it.

"We have not men enough to rebuild it," Kossil replied.

"We have men enough to guard it."

"Only slaves. They cannot be trusted."

"They can be trusted if they're frightened. Let the penalty be the same for them as for the stranger they allow to set foot on the holy ground within the wall."

"What is that penalty?" Kossil did not ask to learn the answer. She had taught the answer to Arha, long ago.

"To be decapitated before the Throne."

"Is it my mistress' will that a guard be set upon the Tomb Wall?"

"It is," the girl answered. Inside her long black sleeves her fingers clenched with elation. She knew Kossil did not want to spare a slave to this duty of watching the wall, and indeed it was a useless duty, for what strangers ever came here? It was not likely that any man would wander, by mischance or intent, anywhere within a mile of the Place without being seen; he certainly would get nowhere near the Tombs. But a guard was an honor due them, and Kossil could not well argue against it. She must obey Arha.

"Here," said her cold voice.

Arha stopped. She had often walked this path around the Tomb Wall, and knew it as she knew every foot of the Place, every rock and thorn and thistle. The great rock wall reared up thrice her height to the left; to the right the hill shelved away into a shallow, arid valley, which soon rose again towards the foothills of the western range. She looked over all the ground nearby, and saw nothing that she had not seen before.

"Under the red rocks, mistress."

A few yards down the slope an outcropping of red lava made a stair or little cliff in the hill. When she went down to it and stood on the level before it, facing the rocks, Arha realized that they looked like a rough doorway, four feet high.

"What must be done?"

She had learned long ago that in the holy places it is no use trying to open a door until you know how the door is opened.

"My mistress has all the keys to the dark places."

Since the rites of her coming of age, Arha had worn on her belt an iron ring on which hung a little dagger and thirteen keys, some long and heavy, some small as fishhooks. She lifted the ring and spread the keys. "That one," Kossil said, pointing; and then placed her thick forefinger on a crevice between two red, pitted rock-surfaces.

The key, a long shaft of iron with two ornate wards, entered the crevice. Arha turned it to the left, using both hands, for it was stiff to move; yet it turned smoothly.

"Now?"

"Together—"

Together they pushed at the rough rock face to the left of the keyhole. Heavily, but without catch and with very little noise, an uneven section of the red rock moved inward until a narrow slit was opened. Inside it was blackness.

Arha stooped and entered.

Kossil, a heavy woman heavily clothed, had to squeeze through the narrow opening. As soon as she was inside she backed against the door and, straining, pushed it shut.

It was absolutely black. There was no light. The dark seemed to press like wet felt upon the open eyes.

They crouched, almost doubled over, for the place they stood in was not four feet high, and so narrow that Arha's groping hands touched damp rock at once to right and left.

"Did you bring a light?"

She whispered, as one does in the dark.

"I brought no light," Kossil replied, behind her. Kossil's voice too was lowered, but it had an odd sound to it, as if she were smiling. Kossil never smiled. Arha's heart jumped; the blood pounded in her throat. She said to herself, fiercely: This is my place, I belong here, I will not be afraid!

Aloud she said nothing. She started forward; there was only one way to go. It went into the hill, and downward.

Kossil followed, breathing heavily, her garments brushing and scraping against rock and earth.

All at once the roof lifted: Arha could stand straight,

and stretching out her hands she felt no walls. The air, which had been close and earthy, touched her face with a cooler dampness, and faint movements in it gave the sense of a great expanse. Arha took a few cautious steps forward into the utter blackness. A pebble, slipping under her sandaled foot, struck another pebble, and the tiny sound wakened echoes, many echoes, minute, remote, yet more remote. The cavern must be immense, high and broad, yet not empty: something in its darkness, surfaces of invisible objects or partitions, broke the echo into a thousand fragments.

"Here we must be beneath the Stones," the girl said whispering, and her whisper ran out into the hollow blackness and frayed into threads of sound as fine as spiderweb, that clung to the hearing for a long time.

"Yes. This is the Undertomb. Go on. I cannot stay here. Follow the wall to the left. Pass three openings."

Kossil's whisper hissed (and the tiny echoes hissed after it). She was afraid, she was indeed afraid. She did not like to be here among the Nameless Ones, in their tombs, in their caves, in the dark. It was not her place, she did not belong here.

"I shall come here with a torch," Arha said, guiding herself along the wall of the cavern by the touch of her fingers, wondering at the strange shapes of the rock, hollows and swellings and fine curves and edges, rough as lace here, smooth as brass there: surely this was carven work. Perhaps the whole cavern was the work of sculptors of the ancient days?

"Light is forbidden here." Kossil's whisper was sharp. Even as she said it, Arha knew it must be so. This was the very home of darkness, the inmost center of the night.

Three times her fingers swept across a gap in the complex, rocky blackness. The fourth time she felt for the height and width of the opening, and entered it. Kossil came behind.

In this tunnel, which went upward again at a slight slant, they passed an opening on the left, and then at a branching way took the right: all by feel, by groping, in the blindness of the underearth and the silence inside the ground. In such a passageway as this, one must reach out almost constantly to touch both sides of the tunnel, lest one of the openings that must be counted be missed, or the forking of the way go unnoticed. Touch was one's whole guidance; one could not see the way, but held it in one's hands.

"Is this the Labyrinth?"

"No. This is the lesser maze, which is beneath the Throne."

"Where is the entrance to the Labyrinth?"

Arha liked this game in the dark, she wanted a greater puzzle to be set her.

"The second opening we passed in the Undertomb. Feel for a door to the right now, a wooden door, perhaps we've passed it already—"

Arha heard Kossil's hands fumbling uneasily along the wall, scraping on the rough rock. She kept her fingertips light against the rock, and in a moment felt the smooth grain of wood beneath them. She pushed on it, and the door creaked open easily. She stood for a moment blind with light.

They entered a large low room, walled with hewn stone and lighted by one fuming torch hung from a chain. The place was foul with the torch-smoke that had no outlet. Arha's eyes stung and watered.

"Where are the prisoners?"

"There."

At last she realized that the three heaps of something on the far side of the room were men.

"The door isn't locked. Is there no guard?"

"None is needed."

She went a little farther into the room, hesitant, peering through the smoky haze. The prisoners were manacled by both ankles and one wrist to great rings driven into the rock of the wall. If one of them wanted to lie down, his chained arm must remain raised, hanging from the manacle. Their hair and beards had made a matted tangle which, together with the shadows, hid their faces. One of them half lay, the other two sat or squatted. They were naked. The smell from them was stronger even than the reek of smoke.

One of them seemed to be watching Arha; she thought she saw the glitter of eyes, then was not sure. The others had not moved or lifted their heads.

She turned away. "They are not men any more," she said.

"They were never men. They were demons, beast-spirits, who plotted against the sacred life of the God-king!" Kossil's eyes shone with the reddish torchlight.

Arha looked again at the prisoners, awed and curious. "How could a man attack a god? How was it? You: how could you dare attack a living god?"

The one man stared at her through the black brush of his hair, but said nothing.

"Their tongues were cut out before they were sent from Awabath," Kossil said. "Do not speak to them, mistress. They are defilement. They are yours, but not to speak to, nor to look at, nor to think upon. They are yours to give to the Nameless Ones."

"How are they to be sacrificed?"

Arha no longer looked at the prisoners. She faced Kossil instead, drawing strength from the massive body, the cold voice. She felt dizzy, and the reek of smoke and filth made her sick, yet she seemed to think and speak with perfect calm. Had she not done this many times before?

"The Priestess of the Tombs knows best what manner of death will please her Masters, and it is hers to choose. There are many ways."

"Let Gobar the captain of the guards hew off their heads. And the blood will be poured out before the Throne."

"As if it were a sacrifice of goats?" Kossil seemed to be sneering at her lack of imagination. She stood dumb. Kossil went on, "Besides, Gobar is a man. No man can enter the Dark Places of the Tombs, surely my mistress remembers that? If he enters, he does not leave. . . ."

"Who brought them here? Who feeds them?"

"The wardens who serve my temple, Duby and Uahto; they are eunuchs and may enter here on the services of the Nameless Ones, as I may. The God-king's soldiers left the prisoners bound outside the wall,

and I and the wardens brought them in through the
Prisoner's Door, the door in the red rocks. So it is always done. The food and water is lowered from a
trapdoor in one of the rooms behind the Throne."

Arha looked up and saw, beside the chain from
which the torch hung, a wooden square set into the
stone ceiling. It was far too small for a man to crawl
through, but a rope lowered from it would come down
just within reach of the middle prisoner of the three.
She looked away again quickly.

"Let them not bring any more food or water, then.
Let the torch go out."

Kossil bowed. "And the bodies, when they die?"

"Let Duby and Uahto bury them in the great cavern
that we passed through, the Undertomb," the girl said,
her voice becoming quick and high. "They must do it
in the dark. My Masters will eat the bodies."

"It shall be done."

"Is this well, Kossil?"

"It is well, mistress."

"Then let us go," Arha said, very shrill. She turned
and hurried back to the wooden door, and out of the
Room of Chains into the blackness of the tunnel. It
seemed sweet and peaceful as a starless night, silent,
without sight, or light, or life. She plunged into the
clean darkness, hurried forward through it like a swim-
mer through water. Kossil hastened along, behind her
and getting farther behind, panting, lumbering. Without
hesitation Arha repeated the missed and taken turnings
as they had come, skirted the vast echoing Undertomb,
and crept, bent over, up the last long tunnel to the shut
door of rock. There she crouched down and felt for the
long key on the ring at her waist. She found it, but
could not find the keyhole. There was no pinprick of
light in the invisible wall before her. Her fingers groped
over it seeking lock or bolt or handle and finding nothing. Where must the key go? How could she get out?

"Mistress!"

Kossil's voice, magnified by echoes, hissed and
boomed far behind her.

"Mistress, the door will not open from inside. There is no way out. There is no return."

Arha crouched against the rock. She said nothing.

"Arha!"

"I am here."

"Come!"

She came, crawling on hands and knees along the passage, like a dog, to Kossil's skirts.

"To the right. Hurry! I must not linger here. It is not my place. Follow me."

Arha got to her feet, and held onto Kossil's robes. They went forward, following the strangely carven wall of the cavern to the right for a long way, then entering a black gap in the blackness. They went upward now, in tunnels, by stairs. The girl still clung to the woman's robe. Her eyes were shut.

There was light, red through her eyelids. She thought it was the torchlit room full of smoke again, and did not open her eyes. But the air smelt sweetish, dry and moldy, a familiar smell; and her feet were on a staircase steep almost as a ladder. She let go Kossil's robe, and looked. A trapdoor was open over her head. She scrambled through it after Kossil. It let her into a room she knew, a little stone cell containing a couple of chests and iron boxes, in the warren of rooms behind the Throne Room of the Hall. Daylight glimmered gray and faint in the hallway outside its door.

"The other, the Prisoner's Door, leads only into the tunnels. It does not lead out. This is the only way out. If there is any other way I do not know of it, nor does Thar. You must remember it for yourself, if there is one. But I do not think there is." Kossil still spoke in an undertone, and with a kind of spitefulness. Her heavy face within the black cowl was pale, and damp with sweat.

"I don't remember the turnings to this way out."

"I'll tell them to you. Once. You must remember them. Next time I will not come with you. This is not my place. You must come alone."

The girl nodded. She looked up into the older woman's face, and thought how strange it looked, pale with scarcely mastered fear and yet triumphant, as if Kossil gloated over her weakness.

"I will come alone after this," Arha said, and then trying to turn away from Kossil she felt her legs give way, and saw the room turn over. She fainted in a little black heap at the priestess' feet.

"You'll learn," Kossil said, still breathing heavily, standing motionless. "You'll learn."

Dreams and Tales

Arha was not well for several days. They treated her
for fever. She kept to her bed, or sat in the mild autumn sunlight on the porch of the Small House, and
looked up at the western hills. She felt weak and stupid. The same ideas occurred to her again and again.
She was ashamed of having fainted. No guard had been
set upon the Tomb Wall, but now she would never
dare ask Kossil about that. She did not want to see
Kossil at all: never. It was because she was ashamed of
having fainted.

Often, in the sunlight, she would plan how she was
going to behave next time she went into the dark places
under the hill. She thought many times about what
kind of death she should command for the next set of
prisoners, more elaborate, better suited to the rituals of
the Empty Throne.

Each night, in the dark, she woke up screaming, "They aren't dead yet! They are still dying!"

She dreamed a great deal. She dreamed that she had to cook food, great cauldrons full of savory porridge, and pour it all out into a hole in the ground. She dreamed that she had to carry a full bowl of water, a deep brass bowl, through the dark, to someone who was thirsty. She could never get to this person. She woke, and she herself was thirsty, but she did not go and get a drink. She lay awake, eyes open, in the room without windows.

One morning Penthe came to see her. From the porch Arha saw her approach the Small House with a careless, purposeless air, as if she just happened to be wandering that way. If Arha had not spoken she would not have come up the steps. But Arha was lonely, and spoke.

Penthe made the deep bow required of all who approached the Priestess of the Tombs, and then plopped down on the steps below Arha and made a noise like "Phewph!" She had gotten quite tall and plump; anything she did turned her cherry pink, and she was pink now from walking.

"I heard you were ill. I saved you out some apples." She suddenly produced a rush net containing six or eight perfect yellow apples, from somewhere under her voluminous black robe. She was now consecrated to the service of the Godking, and served in his temple under Kossil; but she wasn't yet a priestess, and still did lessons and chores with the novices. "Poppe and I sorted the apples this year, and I saved the very best ones out. They always dry all the really good ones. Of course they keep best, but it seems such a waste. Aren't they pretty?"

Arha felt the pale gold satin skins of the apples, looked at the twigs to which brown leaves still delicately clung. "They are pretty."

"Have one," said Penthe.

"Not now. You do."

Penthe selected the smallest, out of politeness, and ate it in about ten juicy, skillful, interested bites.

"I could eat all day," she said. "I never get enough. I wish I could be a cook instead of a priestess. I'd cook better than that old skinflint Nathabba, and besides, I'd get to lick the pots. . . . Oh, did you hear about Munith? She was supposed to be polishing those brass pots they keep the rose oil in, you know, those long thin sort of jars with stoppers. And she thought she was supposed to clean the insides too, so she stuck her hand in, with a rag around it, you know, and then she couldn't get it out. She tried so hard it got all puffed up and swollen at the wrist, you know, so that she really *was* stuck. And she went galloping all over the dormitories yelling, 'I can't get it off! I can't get it off!' And Punti's so deaf now he thought it was a fire, and started screeching at the other wardens to come and rescue the novices. And Uahto was milking and came running out of the pen to see what was the matter, and left the gate open, and all the milch-goats got out and came charging into the courtyard and ran into Punti and the wardens and the little girls, and Munith waving this brass pot around on the end of her arm and having hysterics, and they were all sort of rushing around down there when Kossil came down from the temple. And she said, 'What's this? What's this?' "

Penthe's fair, round face took on a repulsive sneer, not at all like Kossil's cold expression, and yet somehow so like Kossil that Arha gave a snort of almost terrified laughter.

" 'What's this? What's all this?' Kossil said. And then—and then the brown goat *butted* her—" Penthe dissolved in laughter, tears welled in her eyes. "And M-Munith hit the, the goat with the p-p-pot—"

Both girls rocked back and forth in spasms of giggling, holding their knees, choking.

"And Kossil turned around and said, 'What's this? What's this?' to the—to the—to the goat. . . ." The end of the tale was lost in laughter. Penthe finally wiped her eyes and nose, and absentmindedly started on another apple.

To laugh so hard made Arha feel a little shaky. She

calmed herself down, and after a while asked, "How did you come here, Penthe?"

"Oh, I was the sixth girl my mother and father had, and they just couldn't bring up so many and marry them all off. So when I was seven they brought me to the Godking's temple and dedicated me. That was in Ossawa. They had too many novices there, I guess, because pretty soon they sent me on here. Or maybe they thought I'd make a specially good priestess or something. But they were wrong about that!" Penthe bit her apple with a cheerful, rueful face.

"Would you rather not have been a priestess?"

"Would I rather! Of course! I'd rather marry a pigherd and live in a ditch. I'd rather anything than stay buried alive here all my born days with a mess of women in a perishing old desert where nobody ever comes! But there's no good *wishing* about it, because I've been consecrated now and I'm stuck with it. But I do hope that in my next life I'm a dancing-girl in Awabath! Because I will have earned it."

Arha looked down at her with a dark steady gaze. She did not understand. She felt that she had never seen Penthe before, never looked at her and seen her, round and full of life and juice as one of her golden apples, beautiful to see.

"Doesn't the Temple mean anything to you?" she asked, rather harshly.

Penthe, always submissive and easily bullied, did not take alarm this time. "Oh, I know your Masters are very important to you," she said with an indifference that shocked Arha. "That makes some sense, anyhow, because you're their one special servant. You weren't just consecrated, you were specially born. But look at me. Am I supposed to feel so much awe and so on about the Godking? After all he's just a man, even if he does live in Awabath in a palace ten miles around with gold roofs. He's about fifty years old, and he's bald. You can see in all the statues. And I'll bet you he has to cut his toenails, just like any other man. I know perfectly well that he's a god, too. But what I think is, he'll be much godlier after he's *dead*."

Arha agreed with Penthe, for secretly she had come to consider the self-styled Divine Emperors of Kargad as upstarts, false gods trying to filch the worship due to the true and everlasting Powers. But there was something underneath Penthe's words with which she didn't agree, something wholly new to her, frightening to her. She had not realized how very different people were, how differently they saw life. She felt as if she had looked up and suddenly seen a whole new planet hanging huge and populous right outside the window, an entirely strange world, one in which the gods did not matter. She was scared by the solidity of Penthe's unfaith. Scared, she struck out.

"That's true. My Masters have been dead a long, long time; and they were never men. . . . Do you know, Penthe, I could call you into the service of the Tombs." She spoke pleasantly, as if offering her friend a better choice.

The pink went right out of Penthe's cheeks.

"Yes," she said, "you could. But I'm not . . . I'm not the sort that would be good at that."

"Why?"

"I am afraid of the dark," Penthe said in a low voice.

Arha made a little sound of scorn, but she was pleased. She had made her point. Penthe might disbelieve in the gods, but she feared the unnameable powers of the dark—as did every mortal soul.

"I wouldn't do that unless you wanted to, you know," Arha said.

A long silence fell between them.

"You're getting to be more and more like Thar," Penthe said in her soft dreamy way. "Thank goodness you're not getting like Kossil! But you're so strong. I wish I were strong. I just like eating. . . ."

"Go ahead," Arha said, superior and amused, and Penthe slowly consumed a third apple down to the seeds.

The demands of the endless ritual of the Place brought Arha out of her privacy a couple of days later. Twin kids had been born out of season to a she-goat, and were to be sacrificed to the Twin God-Brothers as the custom was: an important rite, at which the First Priestess must be present. Then it was dark of the moon, and the ceremonies of the darkness must be performed before the Empty Throne. Arha breathed in the drugging fumes of herbs burning in broad trays of bronze before the Throne, and danced, solitary in black. She danced for the unseen spirits of the dead and the unborn and as she danced the spirits crowded the air around her, following the turn and spin of her feet and the slow, sure gestures of her arms. She sang the songs whose words no man understood, which she had learned syllable by syllable, long ago, from Thar. A choir of priestesses hidden in the dusk behind the great double row of columns echoed the strange words after her, and the air in the vast ruinous room hummed with voices, as if the crowding spirits repeated the chants again and again.

The Godking in Awabath sent no more prisoners to the Place, and gradually Arha ceased to dream of the three now long since dead and buried in shallow graves in the great cavern under the Tombstones.

She summoned up her courage to return to that cavern. She must go back there: the Priestess of the Tombs must be able to enter her own domain without terror, to know its ways.

The first time she entered the trapdoor was hard; yet not so hard as she had feared. She had schooled herself up to it so well, had so determined that she would go alone and keep her nerve, that when she came there she was almost dismayed to find that there was nothing to be afraid of. Graves might be there, but she could not see them; she could not see anything. It was black; it was silent. And that was all.

Day after day she went there, always entering by the trapdoor in the room behind the Throne, until she knew well the whole circuit of the cavern, with its strange sculptured walls—as well as one can know what one cannot see. She never left the walls, for in striking out across the great hollow she might soon lose the sense of direction in the darkness, and so, blundering back at last to the wall, not know where she was. For as she had learned the first time, the important thing down in the dark places was to know which turnings and openings one had passed, and which were to come. It must be done by counting, for they were all alike to the groping hands. Arha's memory had been well trained, and she found no difficulty to this odd trick of finding one's way by touch and number, instead of by sight and common sense. She soon knew by heart all the corridors that opened off the Undertomb, the lesser maze that lay under the Hall of the Throne and the hilltop. But there was one corridor she never entered: the second left of the red rock entrance, that one which, if she entered mistaking it for one she knew, she might never find her way out of again. Her longing to enter it, to learn the Labyrinth, grew steadily, but she restrained it until she had learned all she could about it, aboveground.

Thar knew little about it but the names of certain of its rooms, and the list of directions, of turns made and missed, for getting to these rooms. She would tell these to Arha, but she would never draw them in the dust or even with the gesture of a hand in the air; and she herself had never followed them, had never entered the Labyrinth. But when Arha asked her, "What is the way from the iron door that stands open to the Painted Room?" or, "How does the way run from the Room of Bones to the tunnel by the river?"—then Thar would be silent a little, and then recite the strange directions she had learned long before from Arha-that-was: so many crossings passed, so many left-hand turns taken, and so on, and so on. And all these Arha got by heart, as Thar had, often on the first listening. When she lay in bed nights she would repeat them to herself, trying to imagine the places, the rooms, the turnings.

Thar showed Arha the many spy holes that opened into the maze, in every building and temple of the Place, and even under rocks out of doors. The spider-web of stone-walled tunnels underlay all the Place and even beyond its walls; there were miles of tunnels, down there in the dark. No person there but she, the two High Priestesses, and their special servants, the eunuchs Manan, Uahto, and Duby, knew of the existence of this maze that lay beneath every step they took. There were vague rumors of it among the others; they all knew that there were caves or rooms of some sort under the Tombstones. But none of them was very curious about anything to do with the Nameless Ones and the places sacred to them. Perhaps they felt that the less they knew, the better. Arha of course had been intensely curious, and knowing that there were spy holes into the Labyrinth, had sought for them; yet they were so well concealed, in the pavements of the floors or in the desert ground, that she had never found one, not even the one in her own Small House, until Thar showed it to her.

One night in early spring she took a candle lantern and went down with it, unlit, through the Undertomb to the second passage to the left of the passage from the red rock door.

In the dark, she went some thirty paces down the passage, and then passed through a doorway, feeling the iron frame set in the rock: the limit, until now, of her explorations. Past the Iron Door she went a long way along the tunnel, and when at last it began to curve to the right, she lit her candle and looked about her. For light was permitted, here. She was no longer in the Undertomb. She was in a place less sacred though perhaps more dreadful. She was in the Labyrinth.

The raw, blank walls and vault and floor of rock surrounded her in the small sphere of candlelight. The air was dead. Before her and behind her the tunnel stretched off into darkness.

All the tunnels were the same, crossing and recrossing. She kept careful count of her turnings and passings, and recited Thar's directions to herself, though she knew them perfectly. For it would not do to get lost in the Labyrinth. In the Undertomb and the short passages around it, Kossil or Thar might find her, or Manan come seeking for her, for she had taken him there several times. Here, none of them had ever been:

only she herself. Little good it would do her if they came to the Undertomb and called aloud, and she was lost in some spiraling tangle of tunnels half a mile away. She imagined how she might hear the echo of voices calling her, echoing down every corridor, and she would try to come to them, but, lost, would only become farther lost. So vividly did she imagine this that she stopped, thinking she heard a distant voice calling. But there was nothing. And she would not get lost. She was very careful; and this was her place, her own domain. The powers of the dark, the Nameless Ones, would guide her steps here, just as they would lead astray any other mortal who dared enter the Labyrinth of the Tombs.

She did not go far into it that first time, but far enough that the strange, bitter, yet pleasurable certainty of her utter solitude and independence there grew strong in her, and led her back, and back again, and each time farther. She came to the Painted Room, and the Six Ways, and followed the long Outmost Tunnel, and penetrated the strange tangle that led to the Room of Bones.

"When was the Labyrinth made?" she asked Thar, and the stern, thin priestess answered, "Mistress, I do not know. No one knows."

"Why was it made?"

"For the hiding away of the treasures of the Tombs, and for the punishment of those who tried to steal those treasures."

"All the treasures I've seen are in the rooms behind the Throne, and the basements under it. What lies in the Labyrinth?"

"A far greater and more ancient treasure. Would you look on it?"

"Yes."

"None but you may enter the Treasury of the Tombs. You may take your servants into the Labyrinth, but not into the Treasury. If even Manan entered there, the anger of the dark would waken; he would not leave the Labyrinth alive. There you must go alone, forever. I know where the Great Treasure is.

You told me the way, fifteen years ago, before you died, so that I would remember and tell you when you returned. I can tell you the way to follow in the Labyrinth, beyond the Painted Room; and the key to the treasury is that silver one on your ring, with a figure of a dragon on the haft. But you must go alone."

"Tell me the way."

Thar told her, and she remembered, as she remembered all that was told her. But she did not go to see the Great Treasure of the Tombs. Some feeling that her will or her knowledge was not yet complete held her back. Or perhaps she wanted to keep something in reserve, something to look forward to, that cast a glamor over those endless tunnels through the dark that ended always in blank walls or bare dusty cells. She would wait awhile before she saw her treasures.

After all, had she not seen them before?

It still made her feel strange when Thar and Kossil spoke to her of things she had seen or said before she died. She knew that indeed she had died, and had been reborn in a new body at the hour of her old body's death: not only once, fifteen years ago, but fifty years ago, and before that, and before that, back down the years and hundreds of years, generation before generation, to the very beginning of years when the Labyrinth was dug, and the Stones were raised, and the First Priestess of the Nameless Ones lived in this Place and danced before the Empty Throne. They were all one, all those lives and hers. She was the First Priestess. All human beings were forever reborn, but only she, Arha, was reborn forever as herself. A hundred times she had learned the ways and turnings of the Labyrinth and had come to the hidden room at last.

Sometimes she thought she remembered. The dark places under the hill were so familiar to her, as if they were not only her domain, but her home. When she breathed in the drug-fumes to dance at dark of the moon, her head grew light and her body was no longer hers; then she danced across the centuries, barefoot in black robes, and knew that the dance had never ceased.

Yet it was always strange when Thar said, "You told me before you died . . ."

Once she asked, "Who were those men that came to rob the Tombs? Did any ever do so?" The idea of robbers had struck her as exciting, but improbable. How would they come secretly to the Place? Pilgrims were very few, fewer even than prisoners. Now and then new novices or slaves were sent from lesser temples of the Four Lands, or a small group came to bring some offering of gold or rare incense to one of the temples. And that was all. Nobody came by chance, or to buy and sell, or to sightsee, or to steal; nobody came but under orders. Arha did not even know how far it was to the nearest town, twenty miles or more; and the nearest town was a small one. The Place was guarded and defended by emptiness, by solitude. Anybody crossing the desert that surrounded it, she thought, would have as much chance of going unseen as a black sheep in a snowfield.

She was with Thar and Kossil, with whom much of her time was spent now when she was not in the Small House or alone under the hill. It was a stormy, cold night in April. They sat by a tiny fire of sage on the hearth in the room behind the Godking's temple, Kossil's room. Outside the doorway, in the hall, Manan and Duby played a game with sticks and counters, tossing a bundle of sticks and catching as many as possible on the back of the hand. Manan and Arha still sometimes played that game, in secret, in the inner courtyard of the Small House. The rattle of dropped sticks, the husky mumbles of triumph and defeat, the small crackle of the fire, were the only sounds when the three priestesses fell silent. All around beyond the walls reached the profound silence of the desert night. From time to time came the patter of a sparse, hard shower of rain.

"Many came to rob the Tombs, long ago; but none ever did so," said Thar. Taciturn as she was, she liked now and then to tell a story, and often did so as part of

Arha's instruction. She looked tonight as if a story might be gotten out of her.

"How would any man dare?"

"*They* would dare," Kossil said. "They were sorcerers, wizard-folk from the Inner Lands. That was before the Godkings ruled the Kargad Lands; we were not so strong then. The wizards used to sail from the west to Karego-At and Atuan to plunder the towns on the coast, loot the farms, even come into the Sacred City Awabath. They came to kill dragons, they said, but they stayed to rob towns and temples."

"And their great heroes would come among us to test their swords," Thar said, "and work their ungodly spells. One of them, a mighty sorcerer and dragonlord, the greatest of them all, came to grief here. It was long ago, very long ago, but the tale is still remembered, and not only in this place. The sorcerer was named Erreth-Akbe, and he was both king and wizard in the West. He came to our lands, and in Awabath he joined with certain Kargish rebel lords, and fought for the rule of the city with the High Priest of the Inmost Temple of the Twin Gods. Long they fought, the man's sorcery against the lightning of the gods, and the temple was destroyed around them. At last the High Priest broke the sorcerer's witching-staff, broke in half his amulet of power, and defeated him. He escaped from the city and from the Kargish lands, and fled clear across Earthsea to the farthest west; and there a dragon slew him, because his power was gone. And since that day the power and might of the Inner Lands has ever waned. Now the High Priest was named Intathin, and he was the first of the house of Tarb, that lineage from which, after the fulfillment of the prophecies and the centuries, the Priest-Kings of Karego-At were descended, and from them, the Godkings of all Kargad. So it is that since the day of Intathin the power and might of the Kargish lands has ever grown. Those who came to rob the Tombs, they were sorcerers, trying and trying to get back the broken amulet of Erreth-Akbe. But it is still here, where the High Priest put it for safekeeping. And so are their bones. . . ." Thar pointed at the ground under her feet.

"Half of it is here," Kossil said.

"And the other half lost forever."

"How lost?" asked Arha.

"The one half, in Intathin's hand, was given by him to the Treasury of the Tombs, where it should lie safe forever. The other remained in the sorcerer's hand, but he gave it before he fled to a petty king, one of the rebels, named Thoreg of Hupun. I do not know why he did so."

"To cause strife, to make Thoreg proud," Kossil said. "And so it did. The descendants of Thoreg rebelled again when the house of Tarb ruled; and yet again they took arms against the first Godking, refusing to acknowledge him as either king or god. They were an accursed, ensorcelled race. They are all dead now."

Thar nodded. "The father of our present Godking, the Lord Who Has Arisen, put down that family of Hupun, and destroyed their palaces. When that was done, the half-amulet, which they had kept ever since the days of Erreth-Akbe and Intathin, was lost. No one knows what became of it. And that was a lifetime ago."

"It was thrown out as trash, no doubt," Kossil said. "They say it doesn't look like anything of value, the Ring of Erreth-Akbe. A curse upon it and upon all the things of the wizardfolk!" Kossil spat into the fire.

"Have you seen the half that is here?" Arha asked of Thar.

The thin woman shook her head. "It is in that treasury to which none may come but the One Priestess. It may be the greatest of all the treasures there; I do not know. I think perhaps it is. For hundreds of years the Inner Lands sent thieves and wizards here to try to steal it back, and they would pass by open coffers of gold, seeking that one thing. It is very long since Erreth-Akbe and Intathin lived, and yet still the story is known and told, both here and in the West. Most things grow old and perish, as the centuries go on and on. Very few are the precious things that remain precious, or the tales that are still told."

Arha brooded awhile and said, "They must have been very brave men, or very stupid, to enter the Tombs. Don't they know the powers of the Nameless Ones?"

"No," Kossil said in her cold voice. "They have no gods. They work magic, and think they are gods themselves. But they are not. And when they die, they are not reborn. They become dust and bone, and their ghosts whine on the wind a little while till the wind blows them away. They do not have immortal souls."

"But what is this magic they work?" Arha asked, enthralled. She did not remember having said once that she would have turned away and refused to look at the ships from the Inner Lands. "How do they do it? What does it do?"

"Tricks, deceptions, jugglery," Kossil said.

"Somewhat more," said Thar, "if the tales be true even in part. The wizards of the West can raise and still the winds, and make them blow whither they will. On that, all agree, and tell the same tale. That is why they are great sailors; they can put the wind of magic in their sails, and go where they will, and hush the storms at sea. And it is said that they can make light at will, and darkness; and change rocks to diamonds, and lead to gold; that they can build a great palace or a whole city in one instant, at least in seeming; that they can turn themselves into bears, or fish, or dragons, just as they please."

"I do not believe all that," said Kossil. "That they are dangerous, subtle with trickery, slippery as eels, yes. But they say that if you take his wooden staff away from a sorcerer, he has no power left. Probably there are evil runes written on the staff."

Thar shook her head again. "They carry a staff, indeed, but it is only a tool for the power they bear within them."

"But how do they get the power?" Arha asked. "Where does it come from?"

"Lies," Kossil said.

"Words," said Thar. "So I was told by one who once had watched a great sorcerer of the Inner Lands, a

Mage as they are called. They had taken him prisoner, raiding to the West. He showed them a stick of dry wood, and spoke a word to it. And lo! it blossomed. And he spoke another word, and lo! it bore red apples. And he spoke one word more, and stick, blossoms, apples, and all vanished, and with them the sorcerer. With one word he had gone as a rainbow goes, like a wink, without a trace; and they never found him on that isle. Was that mere jugglery?"

"It's easy to fool fools," Kossil said.

Thar said no more, avoiding argument; but Arha was loath to have the subject dropped. "What do the wizard-folk look like," she asked, "are they truly black all over, with white eyes?"

"They are black and vile. I have never seen one," Kossil said with satisfaction, shifting her heavy bulk on the low stool and spreading her hands to the fire.

"May the Twin Gods keep them afar," Thar muttered.

"They will never come here again," said Kossil. And the fire sputtered, and the rain spattered on the roof, and outside the gloomy doorway Manan cried shrilly, "Aha! A half for me, a half!"

Light
Under the Hill

As the year was rounding again towards winter, Thar died. In the summer a wasting disease had come upon her; she who had been thin grew skeletal, she who had been grim now did not speak at all. Only to Arha would she talk, sometimes, when they were alone together; then even that ceased, and she went silently into the dark. When she was gone, Arha missed her sorely. If Thar had been stern, she had never been cruel. It was pride she had taught to Arha, not fear.

Now there was only Kossil.

A new High Priestess for the Temple of the Twin Gods would come in spring from Awabath; until then,

Arha and Kossil between them were the rulers of the
Place. The woman called the girl "mistress," and
should obey her if commanded. But Arha learned not
to command Kossil. She had the right to do so, but not
the strength; it would take very great strength to stand
up against Kossil's jealousy of a higher status than her
own, her hatred of anything she herself did not control.

Since Arha had learned (from gentle Penthe) of the
existence of unfaith, and had accepted it as a reality
even though it frightened her, she had been able to
look at Kossil much more steadily, and to understand
her. Kossil had no true worship in her heart of the
Nameless Ones or of the gods. She held nothing sacred
but power. The Emperor of the Kargad Lands now held
the power, and therefore he was indeed a godking in
her eyes, and she would serve him well. But to her the
temples were mere show, the Tombstones were rocks,
the Tombs of Atuan were dark holes in the ground,
terrible but empty. She would do away with the worship of the Empty Throne, if she could. She would do
away with the First Priestess, if she dared.

Arha had come to face even this last fact quite steadily. Perhaps Thar had helped her to see it, though she
had never said anything directly. In the first stages of
her illness, before the silence came upon her, she had
asked Arha to come to her every few days, and had
talked to her, telling her much about the doings of the
Godking and his predecessor, and the ways of Awabath—matters which she should as an important priestess know, but which were not often flattering to the
Godking and his court. And she had spoken of her
own life, and described what the Arha of the previous
life had looked like and done; and sometimes, not often, she had mentioned what might be the difficulties
and dangers of Arha's present life. Not once did she
mention Kossil by name. But Arha had been Thar's
pupil for eleven years, and needed no more than a hint
or a tone to understand, and to remember.

After the gloomy commotion of the Rites of Mourn-
ing was over, Arha took to avoiding Kossil. When the

long works and rituals of the day were done, she went
to her solitary dwelling; and whenever there was time,
she went to the room behind the Throne, and opened
the trapdoor, and went down into the dark. In daytime
and nighttime, for it made no difference there, she
pursued a systematic exploration of her domain. The
Undertomb, with its great weight of sacredness, was
utterly forbidden to any but priestesses and their most
trusted eunuchs. Any other, man or woman, who ven-
tured there would certainly be struck dead by the wrath
of the Nameless Ones. But among all the rules she had
learned, there was no rule forbidding entry to the Labyrinth. There was no need. It could be entered only
from the Undertomb; and anyway, do flies need rules
to tell them not to enter in a spider's web?

So she took Manan often into the nearer regions of
the Labyrinth, that he might learn the ways. He was
not at all eager to go there, but as always he obeyed
her. She made sure that Duby and Uahto, Kossil's eunuchs, knew the way to the Room of Chains and the
way out of the Undertomb, but no more; she never
took them into the Labyrinth. She wanted no one but
Manan, utterly faithful to her, to know those secret
ways. For they were hers, hers alone, forever. She had
begun her full exploration with the Labyrinth. All the
autumn she spent many days walking those endless corridors, and still there were regions of them she had
never come to. There was a weariness in that tracing of
the vast, meaningless web of ways; the legs got tired
and the mind got bored, forever reckoning up the turnings and the passages behind and to come. It was wonderful, laid out in the solid rock underground like the
streets of a great city; but it had been made to weary
and confuse the mortal walking in it, and even its priestess must feel it to be nothing, in the end, but a great
trap.

So, more and more as winter deepened, she turned
her thorough exploration to the Hall itself, the altars,
the alcoves behind and beneath the altars, the rooms of
chests and boxes, the contents of the chests and boxes,

the passages and attics, the dusty hollow under the dome where hundreds of bats nested, the basements and underbasements that were the anterooms of the corridors of darkness.

Her hands and sleeves perfumed with the dry sweetness of a musk that had fallen to powder lying for eight centuries in an iron chest, her brow smeared with the clinging black of cobweb, she would kneel for an hour to study the carvings on a beautiful, time-ruined coffer of cedar wood, the gift of some king ages since to the Nameless Powers of the Tombs. There was the king, a tiny stiff figure with a big nose, and there was the Hall of the Throne with its flat dome and porch columns, carved in delicate relief on the wood by some artist who had been dust for how many hundred years. There was the One Priestess, breathing in the drug-fumes from the trays of bronze and prophesying or advising the king, whose nose was broken off in this frame; the face of the Priestess was too small to have clear features, yet Arha would imagine that the face was her own face. She wondered what she had told the king with the big nose, and whether he had been grateful.

She had favorite places in the Hall of the Throne, as one might have favorite spots to sit in a sunny house. She often went to a little half-loft over one of the robing rooms in the hinder part of the Hall. There ancient gowns and costumes were kept, left from the days when great kings and lords came to worship at the Place of the Tombs of Atuan, acknowledging a domain greater than their own or any man's. Sometimes their daughters, the princesses, had put on these soft white silks, embroidered with topaz and dark amethyst, and had danced with the Priestess of the Tombs. There were little painted ivory tables in one of the treasuries, showing such a dance, and the lords and kings waiting outside the Hall, for then as now no man ever set foot on the ground of the Tombs. But the maidens might come in, and dance with the Priestess, in white silk. The Priestess herself wore rough cloth, homespun black, always,

then and now; but she liked to come and finger the
sweet, soft stuff, rotten with age, the unperishing jewels
tearing from the cloth by their own slight weight. There
was a scent in these chests different from all the musks
and incenses of the temples of the Place: a fresher
scent, fainter, younger.

In the treasure rooms she would spend a night learn-
ing the contents of a single chest, jewel by jewel, the
rusted armor, the broken plumes of helms, the buckles
and pins and brooches, bronze, silver-gilt, and solid
gold.

Owls, undisturbed by her presence, sat on the rafters
and opened and shut their yellow eyes. A bit of starlight shone in between tiles of the roof; or the snow
came sifting down, fine and cold as those ancient silks
that fell to nothing at hand's touch.

One night late in the winter, it was too cold in the
Hall. She went to the trapdoor, raised it, swung down
onto the steps, and closed it above her. She set off
silently on the way she now knew so well, the passage
to the Undertomb. There, of course, she never bore a
light; if she carried a lantern, from going in the Labyrinth or in the dark of night above ground, she extin-
guished it before she came near the Undertomb. She
had never seen that place, never in all the generations
of her priestesshood. In the passage now, she blew out
the candle in the lamp she carried, and without slowing
her pace at all went forward in the pitch dark, easy as a
little fish in dark water. Here, winter or summer, there
was no cold, no heat: always the same even chill, a little damp, changeless. Up above, the great frozen winds
of winter whipped thin snow over the desert. Here
there was no wind, no season; it was close, it was still,
it was safe.

She was going to the Painted Room. She liked sometimes to go there and study the strange wall drawings
that leapt out of the dark at the gleam of her candle:
men with long wings and great eyes, serene and
morose. No one could tell her what they were, there
were no such paintings elsewhere in the Place, but she

thought she knew; they were the spirits of the damned, who are not reborn. The Painted Room was in the Labyrinth, so she must pass through the cavern beneath the Tombstones first. As she approached it down the slanting passage, a faint gray bloomed, a bare hint and glimmer, the echo of an echo of a distant light.

She thought her eyes were tricking her, as they often did in that utter blackness. She closed them, and the glimmering vanished. She opened them, and it reappeared.

She had stopped and was standing still. Gray, not black. A dull edge of pallor, just visible, where nothing could be visible, where all must be black.

She took a few steps forward and put out her hand to that angle of the tunnel wall; and, infinitely faint, saw the movement of her hand.

She went on. This was strange beyond thought, beyond fear, this faint blooming of light where no light had ever been, in the inmost grave of darkness. She went noiseless on bare feet, black-clothed. At the last turn of the corridor she halted; then very slowly took the last step, and looked, and saw.

—Saw what she had never seen, not though she had lived a hundred lives: the great vaulted cavern beneath the Tombstones, not hollowed by man's hand but by the powers of the Earth. It was jeweled with crystals and ornamented with pinnacles and filigrees of white limestone where the waters under earth had worked, eons since: immense, with glittering roof and walls, sparkling, delicate, intricate, a palace of diamonds, a house of amethyst and crystal, from which the ancient darkness had been driven out by glory.

Not bright, but dazzling to the dark-accustomed eye, was the light that worked this wonder. It was a soft gleam, like marshlight, that moved slowly across the cavern, striking a thousand scintillations from the jeweled roof and shifting a thousand fantastic shadows along the carven walls.

The light burned at the end of a staff of wood, smokeless, unconsuming. The staff was held by a human hand. Arha saw the face beside the light; the dark face: the face of a man.

She did not move.

For a long time he crossed and recrossed the vast cave. He moved as if he sought something, looking behind the lacy cataracts of stone, studying the several corridors that led out of the Undertomb, yet not entering them. And still the Priestess of the Tombs stood motionless, in the black angle of the passage, waiting.

What was hardest for her to think, perhaps, was that she was looking at a stranger. She had very seldom seen a stranger. It seemed to her that this must be one of the wardens—no, one of the men from over the wall, a goatherd or guard, a slave of the Place; and he had come to see the secrets of the Nameless Ones, maybe to steal something from the Tombs. . . .

To steal something. To rob the Dark Powers. Sacrilege: the word came slowly into Arha's mind. This was a man, and no man's foot must ever touch the soil of the Tombs, the Holy Place. Yet he had come here into the hollow place that was the heart of the Tombs. He had entered in. He had made light where light was forbidden, where it had never been since world's beginning. Why did the Nameless Ones not strike him down?

He was standing now looking down at the rocky floor, which was cut and troubled. One could see that it had been opened and reclosed. The sour sterile clods dug up for the graves had not all been stamped down again.

Her Masters had eaten those three. Why did they not eat this one? What were they waiting for?

For their hands to act, for their tongue to speak. . . .

"Go! Go! Begone!" she screamed all at once at the top of her voice. Great echoes shrilled and boomed across the cavern, seeming to blur the dark, startled face that turned towards her, and, for one moment, across the shaken splendor of the cavern, saw her. Then the light was gone. All splendor gone. Blind dark, and silence.

Now she could think again. She was released from the spell of light.

He must have come in by the red rock door, the Prisoners' Door, so he would try to escape by it. Light and silent as the soft-winged owls she ran the half-circuit of the cavern to the low tunnel that led to the door which opened only inwards. She stooped there at the entrance of the tunnel. There was no draft of wind from outside; he had not left the door fixed open behind him. It was shut, and if he was in the tunnel, he was trapped there.

But he was not in the tunnel. She was sure of it. So close, in that cramped place, she would have heard his breath, felt the warmth and pulse of his life itself. There was no one in the tunnel. She stood erect, and listened. Where had he gone?

The darkness pressed like a bandage on her eyes. To have seen the Undertomb confused her; she was bewildered. She had known it only as a region defined by hearing, by hand's touch, by drifts of cool air in the dark; a vastness; a mystery, never to be seen. She had seen it, and the mystery had given place, not to horror, but to beauty, a mystery deeper even than that of the dark.

She went slowly forward now, unsure. She felt her way to the left, to the second passageway, the one that led into the Labyrinth. There she paused and listened.

Her ears told her no more than her eyes. But, as she stood with one hand on either side of the rock archway, she felt a faint, obscure vibration in the rock, and on the chill, stale air was the trace of a scent that did not belong there: the smell of the wild sage that grew on the desert hills, overhead, under the open sky.

Slow and quiet she moved down the corridor, following her nose.

After perhaps a hundred paces she heard him. He was almost as silent as she, but he was not so sure-footed in the dark. She heard a slight scuffle, as if he had stumbled on the uneven floor and recovered himself at once. Nothing else. She waited awhile and then went slowly on, touching her right hand fingertips very lightly to the wall. At last a rounded bar of metal came under them. There she stopped, and felt up the strip of iron until, almost as high as she could reach, she touched a projecting handle of rough iron. This, suddenly, with all her strength, she dragged downward.

There was a fearful grinding and a clash. Blue sparks leapt out in a falling shower. Echoes died away, quarreling, down the corridor behind her. She put out her hands and felt, only a few inches before her face, the pocked surface of an iron door.

She drew a long breath.

Returning slowly up the tunnel to the Undertomb, and keeping its wall to her right, she went on to the trapdoor in the Hall of the Throne. She did not hasten, and went silently, though there was no need for silence any more. She had caught her thief. The door that he had gone through was the only way into or out of the Labyrinth; and it could be opened only from the outer side.

He was down there now, in the darkness underground, and he would never come out again.

Walking slowly and erect, she went past the Throne into the long columned hall. There, where one bronze bowl on the high tripod brimmed with the red glow of charcoal, she turned and approached the seven steps that led up to the Throne.

On the lowest step she knelt, and bowed her forehead down to the cold, dusty stone, littered with mouse bones dropped by the hunting owls.

"Forgive me that I have seen Your darkness broken," she said, not speaking the words aloud. "Forgive me that I have seen Your tombs violated. You will be avenged. O my Masters, death will deliver him to you, and he will never be reborn!"

Yet even as she prayed, in her mind's eye she saw the quivering radiance of the lighted cavern, life in the place of death; and instead of terror at the sacrilege and rage against the thief, she thought only how strange it was, how strange. . . .

"What must I tell Kossil?" she asked herself as she came out into the blast of the winter wind and drew her cloak about her. "Nothing. Not yet. *I* am mistress of the Labyrinth. This is no business of the Godking's. I'll tell her after the thief is dead, perhaps. How must I kill him? I should make Kossil come and watch him die. She's fond of death. What is it he was seeking? He must be mad. How did he get in? Kossil and I have the only keys to the red rock door and the trapdoor. He must have come by the red rock door. Only a sorcerer could open it. A sorcerer—"

She halted, though the wind almost buffeted her off her feet.

"He is a sorcerer, a wizard of the Inner Lands, seeking the amulet of Erreth-Akbe."

And there was such an outrageous glamor in this, that she grew warm all over, even in that icy wind, and laughed out loud. All around her the Place, and the desert around it, was black and silent; the wind keened; there were no lights down in the Big House. Thin, invisible snow flicked past on the wind.

"If he opened the red rock door with sorcery, he can open others. He can escape."

This thought chilled her for a moment, but it did not convince her. The Nameless Ones had let him enter. Why not? He could not do any harm. What harm is a thief who can't leave the scene of his theft? Spells and black powers he must have, and strong ones no doubt, since he had got that far; but he would not get farther. No spell cast by mortal man could be stronger than the will of the Nameless Ones, the presences in the Tombs, the Kings whose Throne was empty.

To reassure herself of this, she hastened on down to the Small House. Manan was asleep on the porch, rolled up in his cloak and the ratty fur blanket that was his winter bed. She entered quietly, so as not to awaken him, and without lighting any lamp. She opened a little locked room, a mere closet at the end of the hall. She struck a flint spark long enough to find a certain place on the floor, and kneeling, pried up one tile. A bit of heavy, dirty cloth, only a few inches square, was revealed to her touch. This she slipped aside noiselessly. She started back, for a ray of light shot upward, straight into her face.

After a moment, very cautiously, she looked into the opening. She had forgotten that he carried that queer light on his staff. She had been expecting at most to hear him, down there in the dark. She had forgotten the light, but he was where she had expected him to be: right beneath the spy hole, at the iron door that blocked his escape from the Labyrinth.

He was standing there, one hand on his hip, the other holding out at an angle the wooden staff, as tall as he was, to the tip of which clung the soft will-o'-the-wisp. His head, which she looked down upon from some six feet above, was cocked a bit to the side. His clothes were those of any winter traveler or pilgrim, a short heavy cloak, a leather tunic, leggings of wool, laced sandals; there was a light pack on his back, a water bottle slung from it, a knife sheathed at his hip. He stood there still as a statue, easy and thoughtful.

Slowly he raised his staff from the ground, and held the bright tip of it out towards the door, which Arha could not see from her spy hole. The light changed, growing smaller and brighter, an intense brilliance. He spoke aloud. The language he spoke was strange to Arha, but stranger to her than the words was the voice, deep and resonant.

The light on the staff brightened, flickered, dimmed. For a moment it died quite away, and she could not see him.

The pale violet marshlight reappeared, steady, and she saw him turn away from the door. His spell of opening had failed. The powers that held the lock fast on that door were stronger than any magic he possessed.

He looked about him, as if thinking, now what?

The tunnel or corridor in which he stood was about five feet wide. Its roof was from twelve to fifteen feet above the rough rock floor. The walls here were of dressed stone, laid without mortar but very carefully and closely, so that one could scarcely slip a knife-tip into the joints. They leaned inward increasingly as they rose, forming a vault.

There was nothing else.

He started forward. One stride took him out of Arha's range of vision. The light died away. She was about to replace the cloth and the tile, when again the soft shaft of light rose up out of the floor before her. He had come back to the door. Perhaps he had realized that if he once left it and entered the maze, he was not very likely to find it again.

He spoke, one word only, in a low voice. *"Emenn,"* he said, and then again, louder, *"Emenn!"* And the iron door rattled in its jambs, and low echoes rolled down the vaulted tunnel like thunder, and it seemed to Arha that the floor beneath her shook.

But the door stayed fast.

He laughed then, a short laugh, that of a man who thinks, "What a fool I've made of myself!" He looked around the walls once more, and as he glanced upward Arha saw the smile lingering on his dark face. Then he sat down, unslung his pack, got out a piece of dry bread, and munched on it. He unstopped his leather bottle of water and shook it; it looked light in his hand, as if nearly empty. He replaced the stopper without drinking. He put the pack behind him for a pillow, pulled his cloak around him, and lay down. His staff was in his right hand. As he lay back, the little wisp or ball of light floated upward from the staff and hung dimly behind his head, a few feet off the ground. His left hand was on his breast, holding something that hung from a heavy chain around his neck. He lay there quite comfortable, legs crossed at the ankle; his gaze wandered across the spy hole and away; he sighed and closed his eyes. The light grew slowly dimmer. He slept.

The clenched hand on his breast relaxed and slipped aside, and the watcher above saw then what talisman he wore on the chain: a bit of rough metal, crescent-shaped, it seemed.

The faint glimmer of his sorcery died away. He lay in silence and the dark.

Arha replaced the cloth and reset the tile in its place, rose cautiously and slipped away to her room. There she lay long awake in the wind-loud darkness, seeing always before her the crystal radiance that had shimmered in the house of death, the soft unburning fire, the stones of the tunnel wall, the quiet face of the man asleep.

The Man Trap

Next day, when she had finished with her duties at the various temples, and with her teaching of the sacred dances to the novices, she slipped away to the Small House and, darkening the room, opened the spy hole and peered down it. There was no light. He was gone. She had not thought he would stay so long at the una-vailing door, but it was the only place she knew to look. How was she to find him now that he had lost himself?

The tunnels of the Labyrinth, by Thar's account and her own experience, extended in all their windings, branchings, spirals, and dead ends, for more than twenty miles. The blind alley that lay farthest from the Tombs was not much more than a mile away in a straight line, probably. But down underground, nothing ran straight. All the tunnels curved, split, rejoined,

branched, interlaced, looped, traced elaborate routes
that ended where they began, for there was no beginning, and no end. One could go, and go, and go, and
still get nowhere, for there was nowhere to get to.
There was no center, no heart of the maze. And once
the door was locked, there was no end to it. No direction was right.

Though the ways and turnings to the various rooms
and regions were firm in Arha's memory, even she had
taken with her on her longer explorations a ball of fine
yarn, and let it unravel behind her, and rewound it as
she followed it returning. For if one of the turns and
passages that must be counted were missed, even she
might be lost. A light was no help, for there were no
landmarks. All the corridors, all the doorways and
openings, were alike.

He might have gone miles by now, and yet not be
forty feet from the door where he had entered.

She went to the Hall of the Throne, and to the Twin
Gods' temple, and to the cellar under the kitchens, and,
choosing a moment when she was alone, looked
through each of those spy holes down into the cold,
thick dark. When night came, freezing and blazing with
stars, she went to certain places on the Hill and raised
up certain stones, cleared away the earth, peered down
again, and saw the starless darkness underground.

He was there. He must be there. Yet he had escaped
her. He would die of thirst before she found him. She
would have to send Manan into the maze to find him,
once she was sure he was dead. That was unbearable to
think of. As she knelt in the starlight on the bitter
ground of the Hill, tears of rage rose in her eyes.

She went to the path that led back down the slope to
the temple of the Godking. The columns with their
carved capitals shone white with hoarfrost in the starlight, like pillars of bone. She knocked at the rear door,
and Kossil let her in.

"What brings my mistress?" said the stout woman,
cold and watchful.

"Priestess, there is a man within the Labyrinth."

Kossil was taken off guard; for once something had

occurred that she did not expect. She stood and stared. Her eyes seemed to swell a little. It flitted across Arha's mind that Kossil looked very like Penthe imitating Kossil, and a wild laugh rose up in her, was repressed, and died away.

"A man? In the Labyrinth?"

"A man, a stranger." Then as Kossil continued to look at her with disbelief, she added, "I know a man by sight, though I have seen few."

Kossil disdained her irony. "How came a man there?"

"By witchcraft, I think. His skin is dark, perhaps he is from the Inner Lands. He came to rob the Tombs. I found him first in the Undertomb, beneath the very Stones. He ran to the entrance of the Labyrinth when he became aware of me, as if he knew where he went. I locked the iron door behind him. He made spells, but that did not open the door. In the morning he went on into the maze. I cannot find him now."

"Has he a light?"

"Yes."

"Water?"

"A little flask, not full."

"His candle will be burned down already." Kossil pondered. "Four or five days. Maybe six. Then you can send my wardens down to drag the body out. The blood should be fed to the Throne and the—"

"No," Arha said with sudden, shrill fierceness. "I wish to find him alive."

The priestess looked down at the girl from her heavy height. "Why?"

"To make—to make his dying longer. He has committed sacrilege against the Nameless Ones. He has defiled the Undertomb with light. He came to rob the Tombs of their treasures. He must be punished with worse than lying down in a tunnel alone and dying."

"Yes," Kossil said, as if deliberating. "But how will you catch him, mistress? That is chancy. There is no chance about the other. Is there not a room full of bones, somewhere in the Labyrinth, bones of men who entered it and did not leave it? . . . Let the Dark Ones punish him in their own way, in their own ways, the black ways of the Labyrinth. It is a cruel death, thirst."

"I know," the girl said. She turned and went out into the night, pulling her hood up over her head against the hissing, icy wind. Did she not know?

It had been childish of her, and stupid, to come to Kossil. She would get no help there. Kossil herself knew nothing, all she knew was cold waiting and death at the end of it. She did not understand. She did not see that the man must be found. It must not be the same as with those others. She could not bear that again. Since there must be death let it be swift, in daylight. Surely it would be more fitting that this thief, the first man in centuries brave enough to try to rob the Tombs, should die by sword's edge. He did not even have an immortal soul to be reborn. His ghost would go whining through the corridors. He could not be let die of thirst there alone in the dark.

Arha slept very little that night. The next day was filled with rites and duties. She spent the night going, silent and without lantern, from one spy hole to another in all the dark buildings of the Place, and on the windswept hill. She went to the Small House to bed at last, two or three hours before dawn, but still she could not rest. On the third day, late in the afternoon, she walked out alone onto the desert, towards the river that now lay low in the winter drought, with ice among the reeds. A memory had come to her that once, in the autumn, she had gone very far in the Labyrinth, past the Six-Cross, and all along one long curving corridor she had heard behind the stones the sound of running water. Might not a man athirst, if he came that way, stay there? There were spy holes even out here; she had to search for them, but Thar had shown her each one, last year, and she refound them without much trouble. Her recall of place and shape was like that of a blind person: she seemed to feel her way to each hidden spot, rather than to look for it. At the second, the farthest of all from the Tombs, when she pulled up her hood to cut out light, and put her eye to the hole cut in a flat pan of rock, she saw below her the dim glimmer of the wizardly light.

He was there, half out of sight. The spy hole looked down at the very end of the blind alley. She could see only his back, and bent neck, and right arm. He sat near the corner of the walls, and was picking at the stones with his knife, a short dagger of steel with a jeweled grip. The blade of it was broken short. The broken point lay directly under the spy hole. He had snapped it trying to pry apart the stones, to get at the water he could hear running, clear and murmurous in that dead stillness under earth, on the other side of the impenetrable wall.

His movements were listless. He was very different, after these three nights and days, from the figure that had stood lithe and calm before the iron door and laughed at his own defeat. He was still obstinate, but the power was gone out of him. He had no spell to stir those stones aside, but must use his useless knife. Even his sorcerer's light was wan and dim. As Arha watched, the light flickered; the man's head jerked and he dropped the dagger. Then doggedly he picked it up and tried to force the broken blade between the stones.

Lying among ice-bound reeds on the riverbank, unconscious of where she was or what she was doing, Arha put her mouth to the cold mouth of rock, and cupped her hands around to hold the sound in. "Wizard!" she said, and her voice slipping down the stone throat whispered coldly in the tunnel underground.

The man started and scrambled to his feet, so going out of the circle of her vision when she looked for him. She put her mouth to the spy hole again and said, "Go back along the river wall to the second turn. The first turn right, miss one, then right again. At the Six Ways, right again. Then left, and right, and left, and right. Stay there in the Painted Room."

As she moved to look again, she must have let a shaft of daylight shoot through the spy hole into the tunnel for a moment, for when she looked he was back in the circle of her vision and staring upwards at the opening. His face, which she now saw to be scarred in some way, was strained and eager. The lips were parched and black, the eyes bright. He raised his staff, bringing the light closer and closer to her eyes. Frightened, she drew back, stopped the spy hole with its rock lid and litter of covering stones, rose, and went back swiftly to the Place. She found her hands were shaky, and sometimes a giddiness swept over her as she walked. She did not know what to do.

If he followed the directions she had given him, he would come back in the direction of the iron door, to the room of pictures. There was nothing there, no reason for him to go there. There was a spy hole in the ceiling of the Painted Room, a good one, in the treasury of the Twin Gods' temple; perhaps that was why she had thought of it. She did not know. Why had she spoken to him?

She could let a little water for him down one of the spy holes, and then call him to that place. That would keep him alive longer. As long as she pleased, indeed. If she put down water and a little food now and then, he would go on and on, days, months, wandering in the Labyrinth: and she could watch him through the spy holes, and tell him where water was to be found, and sometimes tell him falsely so he would go in vain, but he would always have to go. That would teach him to mock the Nameless Ones, to swagger his foolish manhood in the burial places of the Immortal Dead!

But so long as he was there, she would never be able to enter the Labyrinth herself. Why not? she asked herself, and replied—Because he might escape by the iron door, which I must leave open behind me.... But he could escape no farther than the Undertomb. The truth was that she was afraid to face him. She was afraid of his power, the arts he had used to enter the Undertomb, the sorcery that kept that light burning. And yet, was that so much to be feared? The powers that ruled in the dark places were on her side, not his. Plainly he could not do much, there in the realm of the Nameless Ones. He had not opened the iron door; he had not summoned magic food, nor brought water through the wall, nor conjured up some demon monster to break down the walls, all of which she had feared he might be able to do. He had not even found his way in three days' wandering to the door of the Great Treasury, which surely he had sought. Arha herself had never yet pursued Thar's directions to that room, putting off and putting off the journey out of a certain awe, a reluctance, a sense that the time had not yet come.

Now she thought, why should he not go that journey for her? He could look all he liked at the treasures of the Tombs. Much good they would do him! She could jeer at him, and tell him to eat the gold, and drink the diamonds.

With the nervous, feverish hastiness that had possessed her all these three days, she ran to the Twin Gods' temple, unlocked its little vaulted treasury, and uncovered the well-hidden spy hole in the floor.

The Painted Room was below, but pitch dark. The way the man must follow in the maze was much more roundabout, miles longer perhaps; she had forgotten that. And no doubt he was weakened and not going fast. Perhaps he would forget her directions and take the wrong turning. Few people could remember directions from one hearing of them, as she could. Perhaps he did not even understand the tongue she spoke. If so, let him wander till he fell down and died in the dark, the fool, the foreigner, the unbeliever. Let his ghost whine down the stone roads of the Tombs of Atuan until the darkness ate even it. . . .

Next morning very early, after a night of little sleep and evil dreams, she returned to the spy hole in the little temple. She looked down and saw nothing: blackness. She lowered a candle burning in a little tin lantern on a chain. He was there, in the Painted Room. She saw, past the candle's glare, his legs and one limp hand. She spoke into the spy hole, which was a large one, the size of a whole floor tile: "Wizard!"

No movement. Was he dead? Was that all the strength he had in him? She sneered; her heart pounded. "Wizard!" she cried, her voice ringing in the hollow room beneath. He stirred, and slowly sat up, and looked around bewildered. After a while he looked up, blinking at the tiny lantern that swung from his ceiling. His face was terrible to see, swollen, dark as a mummy's face.

He put his hand out to his staff that lay on the floor beside him, but no light flowered on the wood. There was no power left in him.

"Do you want to see the treasure of the Tombs of Atuan, wizard?"

He looked up wearily, squinting at the light of her lantern, which was all he could see. After a while, with a wince that might have begun as a smile, he nodded once.

"Go out of this room to the left. Take the first corridor to the left. . . ." She rattled off the long series of directions without pause, and at the end said, "There you will find the treasure which you came for. And there, maybe, you'll find water. Which would you rather have now, wizard?"

He got to his feet, leaning on his staff. Looking up with eyes that could not see her, he tried to say something, but there was no voice in his dry throat. He shrugged a little, and left the Painted Room.

She would not give him any water. He would never find the way to the treasure room, anyway. The instructions were too long for him to remember; and there was the Pit, if he got that far. He was in the dark, now. He would lose his way, and would fall down at last and die somewhere in the narrow, hollow, dry halls. And Manan would find him and drag him out. And that was the end. Arha clutched the lip of the spy hole with her hands, and rocked her crouching body back and forth, back and forth, biting her lip as if to bear some dreadful pain. She would not give him any water. She would not give him any water. She would give him death, death, death, death, death.

In that gray hour of her life, Kossil came to her, entering the treasury room with heavy step, bulky in black winter robes.

"Is the man dead yet?"

Arha raised her head. There were no tears in her eyes, nothing to hide.

"I think so," she said, getting up and dusting her skirts. "His light has gone out."

"He may be tricking. The soulless ones are very cunning."

"I shall wait a day to be sure."

"Yes, or two days. Then Duby can go down and bring it out. He is stronger than old Manan."

"But Manan is in the service of the Nameless Ones, and Duby is not. There are places within the Labyrinth where Duby should not go, and the thief is in one of these."

"Why, then it is defiled already—"

"It will be made clean by his death there," Arha said. She could see by Kossil's expression that there must be something strange about her own face. "This is my domain, priestess. I must care for it as my Masters bid me. I do not need more lessons in death."

Kossil's face seemed to withdraw into the black hood, like a desert tortoise's into its shell, sour and slow and cold. "Very well, mistress."

They parted before the altar of the God-Brothers. Arha went, without haste now, to the Small House, and called Manan to accompany her. Since she had spoken to Kossil she knew what must be done.

She and Manan went together up the hill, into the Hall, down into the Undertomb. Straining together at the long handle, they opened the iron door of the Labyrinth. They lit their lanterns there, and entered. Arha led the way to the Painted Room, and from it started on the way to the Great Treasury.

The thief had not got very far. She and Manan had not walked five hundred paces on their tortuous course when they came upon him, crumpled up in the narrow corridor like a heap of rags thrown down. He had dropped his staff before he fell; it lay some distance from him. His mouth was bloody, his eyes half shut.

"He's alive," said Manan, kneeling, his great yellow hand on the dark throat, feeling the pulse. "Shall I strangle him, mistress?"

"No. I want him alive. Pick him up and bring him after me."

"Alive?" said Manan, disturbed. "What for, little mistress?"

"To be a slave of the Tombs! Be still with your talk and do as I say."

His face more melancholy than ever, Manan obeyed, hoisting the young man effortfully up onto his shoulders like a long sack. He staggered along after Arha thus laden. He could not go far at a time under that load. They stopped a dozen times on the return journey for Manan to catch his breath. At each halt the corridor was the same: the grayish-yellow, close-set stones rising to a vault, the uneven rocky floor, the dead air; Manan groaning and panting, the stranger lying still, the two lanterns burning dull in a dome of light that narrowed away into darkness down the corridor in both directions. At each halt Arha dripped some of the water she had brought in a flask into the dry mouth of the man, a little at a time, lest life returning kill him.

"To the Room of Chains?" Manan asked, as they were in the passage that led to the iron door; and at that, Arha thought for the first time where she must take this prisoner. She did not know.

"Not there, no," she said, sickened as ever by the memory of the smoke and reek and the matted, speechless, unseeing faces. And Kossil might come to the Room of Chains "He . . . he must stay in the Labyrinth, so that he cannot regain his sorcery. Where is there a room. . . ."

"The Painted Room has a door, and a lock, and a spy hole, mistress. If you trust him with doors."

"He has no powers, down here. Take him there, Manan."

So Manan lugged him back, half again as far as they had come, too laboring and breathless to protest. When they entered the Painted Room at last, Arha took off her long, heavy winter cloak of wool, and laid it on the dusty floor. "Put him on that," she said.

Manan stared in melancholy consternation, wheezing. "Little mistress—"

"I want the man to live, Manan. He'll die of the cold, look how he shakes now."

"Your garment will be defiled. The Priestess' garment. He is an unbeliever, a man," Manan blurted, his small eyes wrinkling up as if in pain.

"Then I shall burn the cloak and have another woven! Come on, Manan!"

At that he stooped, obedient, and let the prisoner flop off his back onto the black cloak. The man lay still as death, but the pulse beat heavy in his throat, and now and then a spasm made his body shiver as it lay.

"He should be chained," said Manan.

"Does he look dangerous?" Arha scoffed; but when Manan pointed out an iron hasp set into the stones, to which the prisoner could be fastened, she let him go fetch a chain and band from the Room of Chains. He grumbled off down the corridors, muttering the directions to himself; he had been to and from the Painted Room before this, but never by himself.

In the light of her single lantern the paintings on the four walls seemed to move, to twitch, the uncouth human forms with great drooping wings, squatting and standing in a timeless dreariness.

She knelt and let water drop, a little at a time, into the prisoner's mouth. At last he coughed, and his hands reached up feebly to the flask. She let him drink. He lay back with his face all wet, besmeared with dust and blood, and muttered something, a word or two in a language she did not know.

Manan returned at last, dragging a length of iron links, a great padlock with its key, and an iron band which fitted around the man's waist and locked there. "It's not tight enough, he can slip out," he grumbled as he locked the end link onto the ring set in the wall.

"No, look." Feeling less fearful of her prisoner now, Arha showed that she could not force her hand between the iron band and the man's ribs. "Not unless he starves longer than four days."

"Little mistress," Manan said plaintively, "I do not question, but . . . what good is he as a slave to the Nameless Ones? He is a man, little one."

"And you are an old fool, Manan. Come along now, finish your fussing."

The prisoner watched them with bright, weary eyes.

"Where's his staff, Manan? There. I'll take that; it has magic in it. Oh, and this; this I'll take too," and with a quick movement she seized the silver chain that showed at the neck of the man's tunic, and tore it off over his head, though he tried to catch her arms and stop her. Manan kicked him in the back. She swung the chain over him, out of his reach. "Is this your talisman, wizard? Is it precious to you? It doesn't look like much, couldn't you afford a better one? I shall keep it safe for you." And she slipped the chain over her own head, hiding the pendant under the heavy collar of her woolen robe.

"You don't know what to do with it," he said, very hoarse, and mispronouncing the words of the Kargish tongue, but clearly enough.

Manan kicked him again, and at that he made a little grunt of pain and shut his eyes.

"Leave off, Manan. Come."

She left the room. Grumbling, Manan followed.

That night, when all the lights of the Place were out, she climbed the hill again, alone. She filled her flask from the well in the room behind the Throne, and took the water and a big, flat, unleavened cake of buckwheat bread down to the Painted Room in the Labyrinth. She set them just within the prisoner's reach, inside the door. He was asleep, and never stirred. She returned to the Small House, and that night she too slept long and sound.

In early afternoon she returned alone to the Labyrinth. The bread was gone, the flask was dry, the stranger was sitting up, his back against the wall. His face still looked hideous with dirt and scabs, but the expression of it was alert.

She stood across the room from him where he could not possibly reach her, chained as he was, and looked at him. Then she looked away. But there was nowhere particular to look. Something prevented her speaking.

Her heart beat as if she were afraid. There was no reason to fear him. He was at her mercy.

"It's pleasant to have light," he said in the soft but deep voice, which perturbed her.

"What's your name?" she asked, peremptory. Her own voice, she thought, sounded uncommonly high and thin.

"Well, mostly I'm called Sparrowhawk."

"Sparrowhawk? Is that your name?"

"No."

"What is your name, then?"

"I cannot tell you that. Are you the One Priestess of the Tombs?"

"Yes."

"What are you called?"

"I am called Arha."

"The one who has been devoured—is that what it means?" His dark eyes watched her intently. He smiled a little. "What is your name?"

"I have no name. Do not ask me questions. Where do you come from?"

"From the Inner Lands, the West."

"From Havnor?"

It was the only name of a city or island of the Inner Lands that she knew.

"Yes, from Havnor."

"Why did you come here?"

"The Tombs of Atuan are famous among my people."

"But you're an infidel, an unbeliever."

He shook his head. "Oh no, Priestess. I believe in the powers of darkness! I have met with the Unnamed Ones, in other places."

"What other places?"

"In the Archipelago—the Inner Lands—there are places which belong to the Old Powers of the Earth, like this one. But none so great as this one. Nowhere else have they a temple, and a priestess, and such worship as they receive here."

"You came to worship them," she said, jeering.

"I came to rob them," he said.

She stared at his grave face. "Braggart!"

"I knew it would not be easy."

"Easy! It cannot be done. If you weren't an unbeliever you'd know that. The Nameless Ones look after what is theirs."

"What I seek is not theirs."

"It's yours, no doubt?"

"Mine to claim."

"What are you then—a god? a king?" She looked him up and down, as he sat chained, dirty, exhausted. "You are nothing but a thief!"

He said nothing, but his gaze met hers.

"You are not to look at me!" she said shrilly.

"My lady," he said, "I do not mean offense. I am a stranger, and a trespasser. I do not know your ways, nor the courtesies due the Priestess of the Tombs. I am at your mercy, and I ask your pardon if I offend you."

She stood silent, and in a moment she felt the blood rising to her cheeks, hot and foolish. But he was not looking at her and did not see her blush. He had obeyed, and turned away his dark gaze.

Neither spoke for some while. The painted figures all around watched them with sad, blind eyes.

She had brought a stone jug of water. His eyes kept straying to that, and after a time she said, "Drink, if you like."

He hitched himself over to the jug at once, and hefting it as lightly as if it were a wine cup, drank a long, long draft. Then he wet a corner of his sleeve, and cleaned the grime and bloodclot and cobweb off his face and hands as best he could. He spent some while at this, and the girl watched. When he was done he looked better, but his cat-bath had revealed the scars on one side of his face: old scars long healed, whitish on his dark skin, four parallel ridges from eye to jawbone, as if from the scraping talons of a huge claw.

"What is that?" she said. "That scar."

He did not answer at once.

"A dragon?" she said, trying to scoff. Had she not come down here to make mock of her victim, to torment him with his helplessness?

"No, not a dragon."

"You're not a dragonlord, at least, then."

"No," he said rather reluctantly, "I *am* a dragonlord. But the scars were before that. I told you that I had met with the Dark Powers before, in other places of the earth. This on my face is the mark of one of the kinship of the Nameless Ones. But no longer nameless, for I learned his name, in the end."

"What do you mean? What name?"

"I cannot tell you that," he said, and smiled, though his face was grave.

"That's nonsense, fool's babble, sacrilege. They are the Nameless Ones! You don't know what you're talking about—"

"I know even better than you, Priestess," he said, his voice deepening. "Look again!" He turned his head so she must see the four terrible marks across his cheek.

"I don't believe you," she said, and her voice shook.

"Priestess," he said gently, "you are not very old; you can't have served the Dark Ones very long."

"But I have. Very long! I am the First Priestess, the Reborn. I have served my masters for a thousand years and a thousand years before that. I am their servant and their voice and their hands. And I am their vengeance on those who defile the Tombs and look upon what is not to be seen! Stop your lying and your boasting, can't you see that if I say one word my guard will come and cut your head off your shoulders? Or if I go away and lock this door, then nobody will come, ever, and you'll die here in the dark, and those I serve will eat your flesh and eat your soul and leave your bones here in the dust?"

Quietly, he nodded.

She stammered, and finding no more to say, swept out of the room and bolted the door behind her with a clang. Let him think she wasn't coming back! Let him sweat, there in the dark, let him curse and shiver and try to work his foul, useless spells!

But in her mind's eye she saw him stretching out to

sleep, as she had seen him do by the iron door, serene as a sheep in a sunny meadow.

She spat at the bolted door, and made the sign to avert defilement, and went almost at a run towards the Undertomb.

While she skirted its wall on the way to the trapdoor in the Hall, her fingers brushed along the fine planes and traceries of rock, like frozen lace. A longing swept over her to light her lantern, to see once more, just for a moment, the time-carven stone, the lovely glitter of the walls. She shut her eyes tight and hurried on.

The Great Treasure

Never had the rites and duties of the day seemed so many, or so petty, or so long. The little girls with their pale faces and furtive ways, the restless novices, the priestesses whose looks were stern and cool but whose lives were all a secret brangle of jealousies and miseries and small ambitions and wasted passions—all these women, among whom she had always lived and who made up the human world to her, now appeared to her as both pitiable and boring.

But she who served great powers, she the priestess of grim Night, was free of that pettiness. She did not have to care about the grinding meanness of their common life, the days whose one delight was likely to be getting a bigger slop of lamb fat over your lentils than your neighbor got. . . . She was free of the days altogether. Underground, there were no days. There was always and only night.

And in that unending night, the prisoner: the dark man, practicer of dark arts, bound in iron and locked in stone, waiting for her to come or not to come, to bring him water and bread and life, or a knife and a butcher's bowl and death, just as the whim took her.

She had told no one but Kossil about the man, and Kossil had not told anyone else. He had been in the Painted Room three nights and days now, and still she had not asked Arha about him. Perhaps she assumed that he was dead, and that Arha had had Manan carry the body to the Room of Bones. It was not like Kossil to take anything for granted; but Arha told herself that there was nothing strange about Kossil's silence. Kossil wanted everything kept secret, and hated to have to ask questions. And besides, Arha had told her not to meddle in her business. Kossil was simply obeying.

However, if the man was supposed to be dead, Arha could not ask for food for him. So, aside from stealing some apples and dried onions from the cellars of the Big House, she did without food. She had her morning and evening meals sent to the Small House, pretending she wished to eat alone, and each night took the food down to the Painted Room in the Labyrinth, all but the soups. She was used to fasting for a day on up to four days at a time, and thought nothing about it. The fellow in the Labyrinth ate up her meager portions of bread and cheese and beans as a toad eats a fly: snap! it's gone. Clearly he could have done so five or six times over; but he thanked her soberly, as if he were her guest and she his hostess at a table such as she had heard of in tales of feasts at the palace of the Godking, all set with roast meats and buttered loaves and wine in crystal. He was very strange.

"What is it like in the Inner Lands?"

She had brought down a little cross-leg folding stool of ivory, so that she would not have to stand while she questioned him, yet would not have to sit down on the floor, on his level.

"Well, there are many islands. Four times forty, they

say, in the Archipelago alone, and then there are the Reaches; no man has ever sailed all the Reaches, nor counted all the lands. And each is different from the others. But the fairest of them all, maybe, is Havnor, the great land at the center of the world. In the heart of Havnor on a broad bay full of ships is the City Havnor. The towers of the city are built of white marble. The house of every prince and merchant has a tower, so they rise up one above the other. The roofs of the houses are red tile, and all the bridges over the canals are covered in mosaic work, red and blue and green. And the flags of the princes are all colors, flying from the white towers. On the highest of all the towers the Sword of Erreth-Akbe is set, like a pinnacle, skyward. When the sun rises on Havnor it flashes first on that blade and makes it bright, and when it sets the Sword is golden still above the evening, for a while."

"Who was Erreth-Akbe?" she said, sly.

He looked up at her. He said nothing, but he grinned a little. Then as if on second thoughts he said, "It's true you would know little of him here. Nothing beyond his coming to the Kargish lands, perhaps. And how much of that tale do you know?"

"That he lost his sorcerer's staff and his amulet and his power—like you," she answered. "He escaped from the High Priest and fled into the west, and dragons killed him. But if he'd come here to the Tombs, there had been no need of dragons."

"True enough," said her prisoner.

She wanted no more talk of Erreth-Akbe, sensing a danger in the subject. "He was a dragonlord, they say. And you say you're one. Tell me, what is a dragonlord?"

Her tone was always jeering, his answers direct and plain, as if he took her questions in good faith.

"One whom the dragons will speak with," he said, "that is a dragonlord, or at least that is the center of the matter. It's not a trick of mastering the dragons, as most people think. Dragons have no masters. The question is always the same, with a dragon: will he talk with you or will he eat you? If you can count upon his doing the former, and not doing the latter, why then you're a dragonlord."

"Dragons can speak?"

"Surely! In the Eldest Tongue, the language we men learn so hard and use so brokenly, to make our spells of magic and of patterning. No man knows all that language, or a tenth of it. He has not time to learn it. But dragons live a thousand years. . . . They are worth talking to, as you might guess."

"Are there dragons here in Atuan?"

"Not for many centuries, I think, nor in Karego-At. But in your northernmost island, Hur-at-Hur, they say there are still large dragons in the mountains. In the Inner Lands they all keep now to the farthest west, the remote West Reach, islands where no men live and few men come. If they grow hungry, they raid the lands to their east; but that is seldom. I have seen the island where they come to dance together. They fly on their great wings in spirals, in and out, higher and higher over the western sea, like a storming of yellow leaves in autumn." Full of the vision, his eyes gazed through the black paintings on the walls, through the walls and the earth and the darkness, seeing the open sea stretch unbroken to the sunset, the golden dragons on the golden wind.

"You are lying," the girl said fiercely, "you are making it up."

He looked at her, startled. "Why should I lie, Arha?"

"To make me feel like a fool, and stupid, and afraid. To make yourself seem wise, and brave, and powerful, and a dragon-lord and all this and all that. You've seen dragons dancing, and the towers in Havnor, and you know all about everything. And I know nothing at all and haven't been anywhere. But all you know is lies! You are nothing but a thief and a prisoner, and you have no soul, and you'll never leave this place again. It doesn't matter if there's oceans and dragons and white towers and all that, because you'll never see them again, you'll never even see the light of the sun. All I know is the dark, the night underground. And that's all there really is. That's all there is to know, in the end.

The silence, and the dark. You know everything, wizard. But I know one thing—the one true thing!"

He bowed his head. His long hands, copper-brown, were quiet on his knees. She saw the fourfold scar on his cheek. He had gone farther than she into the dark; he knew death better than she did, even death. . . . A rush of hatred for him rose up in her, choking her throat for an instant. Why did he sit there so defenseless and so strong? Why could she not defeat him?

"This is why I have let you live," she said suddenly, without the least forethought. "I want you to show me how the tricks of sorcerers are performed. So long as you have some art to show me, you'll stay alive. If you have none, if it's all foolery and lies, why then I'll have done with you. Do you understand?"

"Yes."

"Very well. Go on."

He put his head in his hands a minute, and shifted his position. The iron belt kept him from ever getting quite comfortable, unless he lay down flat.

He raised his face at last and spoke very seriously. "Listen, Arha. I am a Mage, what you call a sorcerer. I have certain arts and powers. That's true. It's also true that here in the Place of the Old Powers, my strength is very little and my crafts don't avail me. Now I could work illusion for you, and show you all kinds of wonders. That's the least part of wizardry. I could work illusions when I was a child; I can do them even here. But if you believe them, they'll frighten you, and you may wish to kill me if fear makes you angry. And if you disbelieve them, you'll see them as only lies and foolery, as you say; and so I forfeit my life again. And my purpose and desire, at the moment, is to stay alive."

That made her laugh, and she said, "Oh, you'll stay alive awhile, can't you see that? You are stupid! All right, show me these illusions. I know them to be false and won't be afraid of them. I wouldn't be afraid if they were real, as a matter of fact. But go ahead. Your precious skin is safe, for tonight, anyhow."

At that he laughed, as she had a moment ago. They

tossed his life back and forth between them like a ball, playing.

"What do you wish me to show you?"

"What can you show me?"

"Anything."

"How you brag and brag!"

"No," he said, evidently a little stung. "I do not. I didn't mean to, anyway."

"Show me something you think worth seeing. Anything!"

He bent his head and looked at his hands awhile. Nothing happened. The tallow candle in her lantern burned dim and steady. The black pictures on the walls, the bird-winged, flightless figures with eyes painted dull red and white, loomed over him and over her. There was no sound. She sighed, disappointed and somehow grieved. He was weak; he talked great things, but did nothing. He was nothing but a good liar, and not even a good thief. "Well," she said at last, and gathered her skirts together to rise. The wool rustled strangely as she moved. She looked down at herself, and stood up in startlement.

The heavy black she had worn for years was gone; her dress was of turquoise-colored silk, bright and soft as the evening sky. It belled out full from her hips, and all the skirt was embroidered with thin silver threads and seed pearls and tiny crumbs of crystal, so that it glittered softly, like rain in April.

She looked at the magician, speechless.

"Do you like it?"

"Where—"

"It's like a gown I saw a princess wear once, at the Feast of Sunreturn in the New Palace in Havnor," he said, looking at it with satisfaction. "You told me to show you something worth seeing. I show you yourself."

"Make it—make it go away."

"You gave me your cloak," he said as if in reproach. "Can I give you nothing? Well, don't worry. It's only illusion; see."

He seemed not to raise a finger, certainly he said no

word; but the blue splendor of silk was gone, and she stood in her own harsh black.

She stood still awhile.

"How do I know," she said at last, "that you are what you seem to be?"

"You don't," said he. "I don't know what I seem, to you."

She brooded again. "You could trick me into seeing you as——" She broke off, for he had raised his hand and pointed upward, the briefest sketch of a gesture. She thought he was casting a spell, and drew back quickly towards the door; but following his gesture, her eyes found high in the dark arching roof the small square that was the spy hole from the treasury of the Twin Gods' temple.

There was no light from the spy hole; she could see nothing, hear no one overhead there; but he had pointed, and his questioning gaze was on her.

Both held perfectly still for some time.

"Your magic is mere folly for the eyes of children," she said clearly. "It is trickery and lies. I have seen enough. You will be fed to the Nameless Ones. I shall not come again."

She took her lantern and went out, and sent the iron bolts home firm and loud. Then she stopped there outside the door and stood dismayed. What must she do?

How much had Kossil seen or heard? What had they been saying? She could not remember. She never seemed to say what she had intended to say to the prisoner. He always confused her with his talk about dragons, and towers, and giving names to the Nameless, and wanting to stay alive, and being grateful for her cloak to lie on. He never said what he was supposed to say. She had not even asked him about the talisman, which she still wore, hidden against her breast.

That was just as well, since Kossil had been listening.

Well, what did it matter, what harm could Kossil do? Even as she asked herself the question she knew the answer. Nothing is easier to kill than a caged hawk. The man was helpless, chained there in the cage of stone. The Priestess of the Godking had only to send her servant Duby to throttle him tonight; or if she and Duby did not know the Labyrinth this far, all she need do was blow poison-dust down the spy hole into the Painted Room. She had boxes and phials of evil substances, some to poison food or water, some that drugged the air, and killed, if one breathed that air too long. And he would be dead in the morning, and it would all be over. There would never be a light beneath the Tombs again.

Arha hastened through the narrow ways of stone to the entrance from the Undertomb, where Manan waited for her, squatting patient as an old toad in the dark. He was uneasy about her visits to the prisoner. She would not let him come with her all the way, so they had settled on this compromise. Now she was glad that he was there at hand. Him, at least, she could trust.

"Manan, listen. You are to go to the Painted Room, right now. Say to the man that you're taking him to be buried alive beneath the Tombs." Manan's little eyes lit up. "Say that aloud. Unlock the chain, and take him to—" She halted, for she had not yet decided where she could best hide the prisoner.

"To the Undertomb," said Manan, eagerly.

"No, fool. I said to say that, not do it. Wait—"

What place was safe from Kossil and Kossil's spies? None but the deepest places underground, the holiest and most hidden places of the domain of the Nameless, where she dared not come. Yet would Kossil not dare almost anything? Afraid of the dark places she might be, but she was one who would subdue her fear to gain her ends. There was no telling how much of the plan of the Labyrinth she might actually have learned, from Thar, or from the Arha of the previous life, or even from secret explorations of her own in past yeas; Arha suspected her of knowing more than she pretended to know. But there was one way she surely could not have learned, the best-kept secret.

"You must bring the man where I lead you, and you must do it in the dark. Then when I bring you back here, you will dig a grave in the Undertomb, and make

a coffin for it, and put it in the grave empty, and fill in
the earth again, yet so that it can be felt and found if
someone sought for it. A deep grave. Do you understand?"

"No," said Manan, dour and fretful. "Little one, this
trickery is not wise. It is not good. There should not be
a man here! There will come a punishment—"

"An old fool will have his tongue cut out, yes! Do
you dare tell me what is wise? I follow the orders of
the Dark Powers. Follow me!"

"I'm sorry, little mistress, I'm sorry. . . ."

They returned to the Painted Room. There she
waited outside in the tunnel, while Manan entered and
unlocked the chain from the hasp in the wall. She
heard the deep voice ask, "Where now, Manan?" and
the husky alto answer, sullenly, "You are to be buried
alive, my mistress says. Under the Tombstones. Get
up!" She heard the heavy chain crack like a whip.

The prisoner came out, his arms bound with
Manan's leather belt. Manan came behind, holding him
like a dog on a short leash, but the collar was around
his waist and the leash was iron. His eyes turned to
her, but she blew out her candle and without a word
set off into the dark. She fell at once into the slow but
fairly steady pace that she usually kept when she was
not using a light in the Labyrinth, brushing her fingertips very lightly but almost constantly along the walls
on either side. Manan and the prisoner followed behind, much more awkward because of the leash, shuffling and stumbling along. But in the dark they must
go; for she did not want either of them to learn this
way.

A left turn from the Painted Room, and pass two
openings; go right at the Four Ways, and pass the
opening to the right; then a long curving way, and a
flight of steps down, long, slippery, and much too narrow for normal human feet. Farther than these steps
she had never gone.

The air was fouler here, very still, with a sharp odor
to it. The directions were clear in her mind, even the
tones of Thar's voice speaking them. Down the steps

(behind her, the prisoner stumbled in the pitch blackness, and she heard him gasp as Manan kept him afoot with a mighty jerk on the chain), and at the foot of the steps turn at once to the left. Hold the left, then for three openings, then the first right, then hold to the right. The tunnels curved and angled, none ran straight. "Then you must skirt the Pit," said Thar's voice in the darkness of her mind, "and the way is very narrow."

She slowed her step, stooped over, and felt before her with one hand along the floor. The corridor now ran straight for a long way, giving false reassurance to the wanderer. All at once her groping hand, which never ceased to touch and sweep the rock before her, felt nothing. There was a stone lip, an edge: beyond the edge, void. To the right the wall of the corridor plunged down sheer into the pit. To the left there was a ledge or curb, not much more than a hand's breadth wide.

"There is a pit. Face the wall to the left, press against it, and go sideways. Slide your feet. Keep hold of the chain, Manan. . . . Are you on the ledge? It grows narrower. Don't put your weight on your heels. So, I'm past the pit. Reach me your hand. There. . . ."

The tunnel ran in short zigzags with many side openings. From some of these as they passed the sound of their footsteps echoed in a strange way, hollowly; and stranger than that, a very faint draft could be felt, sucking inward. Those corridors must end in pits like the one they had passed. Perhaps there lay, under this low part of the Labyrinth, a hollow place, a cavern so deep and so vast that the cavern of the Undertomb would be little in comparison, a huge black inward emptiness.

But above that chasm, where they went in the dark tunnels, the corridors grew slowly narrower and lower, until even Arha must stoop. Was there no end to this way?

The end came suddenly: a shut door. Going bent over, and a little faster than usual, Arha ran up against it, jarring her head and hands. She felt for the keyhole, then for the small key on her belt-ring, never used, the silver key with the haft shaped like a dragon. It fit, it turned. She opened the door of the Great Treasure of the Tombs of Atuan. A dry, sour, stale air sighed outward through the dark.

"Manan, you may not enter here. Wait outside the door."

"He, but not I?"

"If you enter this room, Manan, you will not leave it. That is the law for all but me. No mortal being but I has ever left this room alive. Will you go in?"

"I will wait outside," said the melancholy voice in the blackness. "Mistress, mistress, don't shut the door—"

His alarm so unnerved her that she left the door ajar. Indeed the place filled her with a dull dread, and she felt some mistrust of the prisoner, pinioned though he was. Once inside, she struck her light. Her hands trembled. The lantern candle caught reluctantly; the air was close and dead. In the yellowish flicker that seemed bright after the long passages of night, the treasure room loomed about them, full of moving shadows.

There were six great chests, all of stone, all thick with a fine gray dust like the mold on bread; nothing else. The walls were rough, the roof low. The place was cold, with a deep and airless cold that seemed to stop the blood in the heart. There were no cobwebs, only the dust. Nothing lived here, nothing at all, not even the rare, small, white spiders of the Labyrinth. The dust was thick, thick, and every grain of it might be a day that had passed here where there was no time or light: days, months, years, ages all gone to dust.

"This is the place you sought," Arha said, and her voice was steady. "This is the Great Treasure of the Tombs. You have come to it. You cannot ever leave it."

He said nothing, and his face was quiet, but there was in his eyes something that moved her: a desolation, the look of one betrayed.

"You said you wanted to stay alive. This is the only place I know where you can stay alive. Kossil will kill you or make me kill you, Sparrowhawk. But here she cannot reach."

Still he said nothing.

"You could never have left the Tombs in any case, don't you see? This is no different. And at least you've come to ... to the end of your journey. What you sought is here."

He sat down on one of the great chests, looking spent. The trailing chain clanked harshly on the stone. He looked around at the gray walls and the shadows, then at her.

She looked away from him, at the stone chests. She had no wish at all to open them. She did not care what marvels rotted in them.

"You don't have to wear that chain, in here." She came to him and unlocked the iron belt, and unbuckled Manan's leather belt from his arms. "I must lock the door, but when I come I will trust you. You know that you *cannot* leave—that you must not try? I am their vengeance, I do their will; but if I fail them—if you fail my trust—then they will avenge themselves. You must not try to leave the room, by hurting me or tricking me when I come. You must believe me."

"I will do as you say," he said gently.

"I'll bring food and water when I can. There won't be much. Water enough, but not much food for a while; I'm getting hungry, do you see? But enough to stay alive on. I may not be able to come back for a day or two days, perhaps even longer. I must get Kossil off the track. But I will come. I promise. Here's the flask. Hoard it, I can't come back soon. But I will come back."

He raised his face to her. His expression was strange. "Take care, Tenar," he said.

Names

She brought Manan back through the winding ways in the dark, and left him in the dark of the Undertomb, to dig the grave that must be there as proof to Kossil that the thief had indeed been punished. It was late, and she went straight to the Small House to bed. In the night she woke suddenly; she remembered that she had left her cloak in the Painted Room. He would have nothing for warmth in that dank vault but his own short cloak, no bed but the dusty stone. A cold grave, a cold grave, she thought miserably, but she was too weary to wake up fully, and soon slipped back into sleep. She began to dream. She dreamt of the souls of the dead on the walls of the Painted Room, the figures like great bedraggled birds with human hands and feet and faces, squatting in the dust of the dark places. They could not fly. Clay was their food and dust their drink. They were the souls of those not reborn, the ancient peoples and the unbelievers, those whom the Nameless Ones devoured. They squatted all around her in the shadows, and a faint creaking or cheeping sound came from them now and then. One of them came up quite close to her. She was afraid at first and tried to draw away, but could not move. This one had the face of a bird, not a human face; but its hair was golden, and it said in a woman's voice, "Tenar," tenderly, softly, "Tenar."

She woke. Her mouth was stopped with clay. She lay in a stone tomb, underground. Her arms and legs were bound with graveclothes and she could not move or speak.

Her despair grew so great that it burst her breast open and like a bird of fire shattered the stone and broke out into the light of day—the light of day, faint in her windowless room.

Really awake this time, she sat up, worn out by that night's dreaming, her mind befogged. She got into her clothes, and went out to the cistern in the walled court-yard of the Small House. She plunged her arms and face, her whole head, into the icy water until her body jumped with cold and her blood raced. Then flinging back her dripping hair she stood erect and looked up into the morning sky.

It was not long past sunrise, a fair winter's day. The sky was yellowish, very clear. High up, so high he caught the sunlight and burned like a fleck of gold, a bird was circling, a hawk or desert eagle.

"I am Tenar," she said, not aloud, and she shook with cold, and terror, and exultation, there under the open, sunwashed sky. "I have my name back. I am Tenar!"

The golden fleck veered westward towards the mountains, out of sight. Sunrise gilded the eaves of the Small House. Sheep bells clanked, down in the folds. The smells of woodsmoke and buckwheat porridge from the kitchen chimneys drifted on the fine, fresh wind.

"I am so hungry. . . . How did he know? How did he know my name? . . . Oh, I've got to go eat, I'm so hungry. . . ."

She pulled up her hood and ran off to breakfast.

Food, after three days of semi-fasting, made her feel solid, gave her ballast; she didn't feel so wild and lighthearted and frightened. She felt quite capable of handling Kossil, after breakfast.

She came up beside the tall, stout figure on the way out of the dining hall of the Big House, and said in a low voice, "I have done away with the robber. . . . What a fine day it is!"

The cold gray eyes looked sidelong at her from the black hood.

"I thought that the Priestess must abstain from eating for three days after a human sacrifice?"

This was true. Arha had forgotten it, and her face showed that she had forgotten.

"He is not dead yet," she said at last, trying to feign the indifferent tone that had come so easily a moment ago. "He is buried alive. Under the Tombs. In a coffin. There will be some air, the coffin isn't sealed, it's a wooden one. It will go quite slowly; the dying. When I know he is dead then I'll begin the fast."

"How will you know?"

Flustered, she hesitated again. "I will know. The . . . My Masters will tell me."

"I see. Where is the grave?"

"In the Undertomb. I told Manan to dig it beneath the Smooth Stone." She must not answer so quickly, in that foolish, appeasing tone; she must be on her dignity with Kossil.

"Alive, in a wooden coffin. That's a risky thing with a sorcerer, mistress. Did you make sure his mouth was stopped so he cannot say charms? Are his hands bound? They can weave spells with the motion of a finger, even when their tongues are cut out."

"There is nothing to his sorcery, it is mere tricking," the girl said, raising her voice. "He is buried, and my Masters are waiting for his soul. And the rest does not concern you, priestess!"

This time she had gone too far. Others could hear; Penthe and a couple of other girls, Duby, and the priestess Mebbeth, all were in hearing distance. The girls were all ears, and Kossil was aware of it.

"All that happens here is my concern, mistress. All that happens in his realm is the concern of the Godking, the Man Immortal, whose servant I am. Even into the places underground and into the hearts of men does he search and look, and none shall forbid him entrance!"

"I shall. Into the Tombs no one comes if the Nameless Ones forbid it. They were before your Godking and they will be after him. Speak softly of them, priestess. Do not call their vengeance on you. They will come into your dreams, they will enter the dark places in your mind, and you will go mad."

The girl's eyes were blazing. Kossil's face was hidden, drawn back into the black cowl. Penthe and the others watched, terrified and enthralled.

"They are old," Kossil's voice said, not loud, a whistling thread of sound out of the depths of the cowl. "They are old. Their worship is forgotten, save in this one place. Their power is gone. They are only shadows. They have no power any more. Do not try to frighten me, Eaten One. You are the First Priestess; does that not mean also that you are the last? ... You cannot trick me. I see into your heart. The darkness hides nothing from me. Take care, Arha!"

She turned and went on, with her massive, deliberate steps, crushing the frost-starred weeds under her heavy, sandaled feet, going to the white-pillared house of the Godking.

The girl stood, slight and dark, as if frozen to earth, in the front courtyard of the Big House. Nobody moved, nothing moved, only Kossil, in all the vast landscape of court and temple, hill and desert plain and mountain.

"May the Dark Ones eat your soul, Kossil!" she shouted in a voice like a hawk's scream, and lifting her arm with the hand stretched out stiff, she brought the curse down on the priestess' heavy back, even as she set foot on the steps of her temple. Kossil staggered, but did not stop or turn. She went on, and entered the Godking's door.

Arha spent that day sitting on the lowest step of the Empty Throne. She dared not go into the Labyrinth; she would not go among the other priestesses. A heaviness filled her, and held her there hour after hour in the cold dusk of the great hall. She stared at the pairs of thick pale columns going off into the gloom at the distant end of the hall, and at the shafts of daylight that slanted in from holes in the roof, and at the thick-curling smoke from the bronze tripod of charcoal near the Throne. She made patterns with the little bones of mice on the marble stair, her head bowed, her mind active and yet as if stupefied. Who am I? she asked herself, and got no answer.

Manan came shuffling down the hall between the double rows of columns, when the light had long since ceased to shaft the hall's darkness, and the cold had grown intense. Manan's doughy face was very sad. He stood at a distance from her, his big hands hanging; a torn hem of his rusty cloak dangled by his heel.

"Little mistress."

"What is it, Manan?" She looked at him with dull affection.

"Little one, let me do what you said ... what you said was done. He must die, little one. He has bewitched you. She will have revenge. She is old and cruel, and you are too young. You have not strength enough."

"She can't hurt me."

"If she killed you, even in the sight of all, in the open, there is none in all the Empire who would dare punish her. She is the High Priestess of the Godking, and the Godking rules. But she won't kill you in the open. She will do it by stealth, by poison, in the night."

"Then I will be born again."

Manan twisted his big hands together. "Perhaps she will not kill you," he whispered.

"What do you mean?"

"She could lock you into a room in the ... down

there. . . . As you have done with him. And you would be alive for years and years, maybe. For years. . . . And no new Priestess would be born, for you wouldn't be dead. Yet there would be no Priestess of the Tombs, and the dances of the dark of the moon would not be danced, and the sacrifices would not be made, and the blood not poured out, and the worship of the Dark Ones could be forgotten, forever. She and her Lord would like it to be so."

"*They* would set me free, Manan."

"Not while they are wrathful at you, little mistress," Manan whispered.

"Wrathful?"

"Because of him. . . . The sacrilege not paid for. Oh little one, little one! They do not forgive!"

She sat in the dust of the lowest step, her head bowed. She looked at a tiny thing that she held on her palm, the minute skull of a mouse. The owls in the rafters over the Throne stirred a little; it was darkening towards night.

"Do not go down into the Labyrinth tonight," Manan said very low. "Go to your house, and sleep. In the morning go to Kossil, and tell her that you lift the curse from her. And that will be all. You need not worry. I will show her proof."

"Proof?"

"That the sorcerer is dead."

She sat still. Slowly she closed her hand, and the fragile skull cracked and collapsed. When she opened her hand it held nothing but splinters of bone and dust.

"No," she said. She brushed the dust from her palm.

"He must die. He has put a spell on you. You are lost, Arha!"

"He has not put any spell on me. You're old and cowardly, Manan; you're frightened by old women. How do you think you'd come to him and kill him and get your 'proof'? Do you know the way clear to the Great Treasure, that you followed in the dark last night? Can you count the turnings and come to the steps, and then the pit, and then the door? Can you unlock that door? . . . Oh, poor old Manan, your wits are all thick. She has frightened you. You go down to the Small House now, and sleep, and forget all these things. Don't worry me forever with talk of death. . . . I'll come later. Go on, go on, old fool, old lump." She had risen, and gently pushed Manan's broad chest, patting him and pushing him to go. "Good night, good night!"

He turned, heavy with reluctance and foreboding, but obedient, and trudged down the long hall under the columns and the ruined roof. She watched him go.

When he had been gone some while she turned and went around the dais of the Throne, and vanished into the dark behind it.

The Ring
of Erreth-Akbe

In the Great Treasury of the Tombs of Atuan, time did not pass. No light; no life; no least stir of spider in the dust or worm in the cold earth. Rock, and dark, and time not passing.

On the stone lid of a great chest the thief from the Inner Lands lay stretched on his back like the carven figure on a tomb. The dust disturbed by his movements had settled on his clothes. He did not move.

The lock of the door rattled. The door opened. Light broke the dead black and a fresher draft stirred the dead air. The man lay inert.

Arha closed the door and locked it from within, set her lantern on a chest, and slowly approached the motionless figure. She moved timorously, and her eyes

103

were wide, the pupils still fully dilated from her long
journey through the dark.

"Sparrowhawk!"

She touched his shoulder, and spoke his name again,
and yet again.

He stirred then, and moaned. At last he sat up,
face drawn and eyes blank. He looked at her unrecog-
nizing.

"It's I, Arha—Tenar. I brought you water. Here,
drink."

He fumbled for the flask as if his hands were numb,
and drank, but not deeply.

"How long has it been?" he asked, speaking with
difficulty.

"Two days have passed since you came to this room.
This is the third night. I couldn't come earlier. I had to
steal the food—here it is—" She got out one of the flat
gray loaves from the bag she had brought, but he
shook his head.

"I'm not hungry. This . . . this is a deathly place."
He put his head in his hands and sat unmoving.

"Are you cold? I brought the cloak from the Painted
Room."

He did not answer.

She put the cloak down and stood gazing at him. She
was trembling a little, and her eyes were still black and
wide.

All at once she sank down on her knees, bowed
over, and began to cry, with deep sobs that wrenched
her body, but brought no tears.

He got down stiffly from the chest, and bent over
her. "Tenar—"

"I am not Tenar. I am not Arha. The gods are dead,
the gods are dead."

He laid his hands on her head, pushing back the
hood. He began to speak. His voice was soft, and the
words were in no tongue she had ever heard. The
sound of them came into her heart like rain falling. She
grew still to listen.

When she was quiet he lifted her, and set her like a

child on the great chest where he had lain. He put his hand on hers.

"Why did you weep, Tenar?"

"I'll tell you. It doesn't matter what I tell you. You can't do anything. You can't help. You're dying too, aren't you? So it doesn't matter. Nothing matters. Kossil, the Priestess of the Godking, she was always cruel, she kept trying to make me kill you. The way I killed those others. And I would not. What right has she? And she defied the Nameless Ones and mocked them, and I set a curse upon her. And since then I've been afraid of her, because it's true what Manan said, she doesn't believe in the gods. She wants them to be forgotten, and she'd kill me while I slept. So I didn't sleep. I didn't go back to the Small House. I stayed in the Hall all last night, in one of the lofts, where the dancing dresses are. Before it was light I went down to the Big House and stole some food from the kitchen, and then I came back to the Hall and stayed there all day. I was trying to find out what I should do. And tonight . . . tonight I was so tired, I thought I could go to a holy place and go to sleep, she might be afraid to come there. So I came down to the Undertomb. That great cave where I first saw you. And . . . and she was there. She must have come in by the red rock door. She was there with a lantern. Scratching in the grave that Manan dug, to see if there was a corpse in it. Like a rat in a graveyard, a great fat black rat, digging. And the light burning in the Holy Place, the dark place. And the Nameless Ones did nothing. They didn't kill her or drive her mad. They are old, as she said. They are dead. They are all gone. I am not a priestess any more."

The man stood listening, his hand still on hers, his head a little bent. Some vigor had come back into his face and stance, though the scars on his cheek showed livid gray, and there was dust yet on his clothes and hair.

"I went past her, through the Undertomb. Her candle made more shadows than light, and she didn't hear me. I wanted to go into the Labyrinth to get away from her. But when I was in it I kept thinking that I heard her following me. All through the corridors I kept hearing somebody behind me. And I didn't know where to go. I thought I would be safe here, I thought my Masters would protect me and defend me. But they don't, they are gone, they are dead. . . ."

"It was for them you wept—for their death? But they are here, Tenar, here!"

"How should you know?" she said listlessly.

"Because every instant since I set foot in the cavern under the Tombstones, I have striven to keep them still, to keep them unaware. All my skills have gone to that, I have spent my strength on it. I have filled these tunnels with an endless net of spells, spells of sleep, of stillness, of concealment, and yet still they are aware of me, half aware; half sleeping, half awake. And even so I am all but worn out, striving against them. This is a most terrible place. One man alone has no hope, here. I was dying of thirst when you gave me water, yet it was not the water alone that saved me. It was the strength of the hands that gave it." As he said that, he turned her hand palm upward in his own for a moment, gazing at it; then he turned away, walked a few steps about the room, and stopped again before her. She said nothing.

"Did you truly think them dead? You know better in your heart. They do not die. They are dark and undying, and they hate the light: the brief, bright light of our mortality. They are immortal, but they are not gods. They never were. They are not worth the worship of any human soul."

She listened, her eyes heavy, her gaze fixed on the flickering lantern.

"What have they ever given you, Tenar?"

"Nothing," she whispered.

"They have nothing to give. They have no power of making. All their power is to darken and destroy. They cannot leave this place; they *are* this place; and it should be left to them. They should not be denied nor forgotten, but neither should they be worshiped. The Earth is beautiful, and bright, and kindly, but that is not all. The Earth is also terrible, and dark, and cruel. The rabbit shrieks dying in the green meadows. The mountains clench their great hands full of hidden fire. There are sharks in the sea, and there is cruelty in men's eyes. And where men worship these things and abase themselves before them, there evil breeds; there places are made in the world where darkness gathers, places given over wholly to the Ones whom we call Nameless, the ancient and holy Powers of the Earth before the Light, the powers of the dark, of ruin, of madness. . . . I think they drove your priestess Kossil mad a long time ago; I think she has prowled these caverns as she prowls the labyrinth of her own self, and now she cannot see the daylight any more. She tells you that the Nameless Ones are dead; only a lost soul, lost to truth, could believe that. They exist. But they are not your Masters. They never were. You are free, Tenar. You were taught to be a slave, but you have broken free."

She listened, though her expression did not change. He said no more. They were silent; but it was not the silence that had been in that room before she entered. There was the breathing of two of them now, and the movement of life in their veins, and the burning of the candle in its lantern of tin, a tiny, lively sound.

"How is it that you know my name?"

He walked up and down the room, stirring up the fine dust, stretching his arms and shoulders in an effort to shake off the numbing chill.

"Knowing names is my job. My art. To weave the magic of a thing, you see, one must find its true name out. In my lands we keep our true names hidden all our lives long, from all but those whom we trust utterly; for there is great power, and great peril, in a name. Once, at the beginning of time, when Segoy raised the isles of Earthsea from the ocean deeps, all things bore their own true names. And all doing of magic, all wizardry, hangs still upon the knowledge— the relearning, the remembering—of that true and ancient language of the Making. There are spells to learn, of course, ways to use the words; and one must know the consequences, too. But what a wizard spends his life at is finding out the names of things, and finding out how to find out the names of things."

"How did you find out mine?"

He looked at her a moment, a deep clear glance across the shadows between them; he hesitated a moment. "I cannot tell you that. You are like a lantern swathed and covered, hidden away in a dark place. Yet the light shines; they could not put out the light. They could not hide you. As I know the light, as I know you, I know your name, Tenar. That is my gift, my power. I cannot tell you more. But tell me this: what will you do now?"

"I don't know."

"Kossil has found an empty grave, by now. What will she do?"

"I don't know. If I go back up, she can have me killed. It is death for a High Priestess to lie. She could have me sacrificed on the steps of the Throne if she wanted. And Manan would have to really cut off my head this time, instead of just lifting the sword and waiting for the Dark figure to stop it. But this time it wouldn't stop. It would come down and cut off my head."

Her voice was dull and slow. He frowned. "If we stay here long," he said, "you are going to go mad, Tenar. The anger of the Nameless Ones is heavy on your mind. And on mine. It's better now that you're here, much better. But it was a long time before you came, and I've used up most of my strength. No one can withstand the Dark Ones long alone. They are very strong." He stopped; his voice had sunk low, and he seemed to have lost the thread of his speech. He rubbed his hands over his forehead, and presently went to drink again from the flask. He broke off a hunch of bread and sat down on the chest opposite to eat it.

What he said was true; she felt a weight, a pressure on her mind, that seemed to darken and confuse all thought and feeling. Yet she was not terrified, as she had been coming through the corridors alone. Only the utter silence outside the room seemed terrible. Why was that? She had never feared the silence of the underearth before. But never before had she disobeyed the Nameless Ones, never had she set herself against them.

She gave a little whimpering laugh at last. "Here we sit on the greatest treasure of the Empire," she said. "The God-king would give all his wives to have one chest of it. And we haven't even opened a lid to look."

"I did," said the Sparrowhawk, chewing.

"In the dark?"

"I made a little light. The werelight. It was hard to do, here. Even with my staff it would have been hard, and without it, it was like trying to light a fire with wet wood in the rain. But it came at last. And I found what I was after."

She raised her face slowly to look at him. "The ring?"

"The half-ring. You have the other half."

"I have it? The other half was lost——"

"And found. I wore it on a chain around my neck. You took it off, and asked me if I couldn't afford a better talisman. The only talisman better than half the Ring of Erreth-Akbe would be the whole. But then, as they say, half a loaf's better than none. So you now have my half, and I have yours." He smiled at her across the shadows of the tomb.

"You said, when I took it, that I didn't know what to do with it."

"That was true."

"And you do know?"

He nodded.

"Tell me. Tell me what it is, the ring, and how you came upon the lost half, and how you came here, and why. All this I must know, then maybe I will see what to do."

"Maybe you will. Very well. What is it, the Ring of Erreth-Akbe? Well, you can see that it's not precious looking, and it's not even a ring. It's too big. An arm-ring, perhaps, yet it seems too small for that. No man knows who it was made for. Elfarran the Fair wore it once, before the Isle of Soléa was lost beneath the sea; and it was old when she wore it. And at last it came into the hands of Erreth-Akbe. . . . The metal is hard silver, pierced with nine holes. There's a design like

waves scratched on the outside, and nine Runes of
Power on the inside. The half you have bears four
runes and a bit of another; and mine likewise. The
break came right across that one symbol, and destroyed
it. It is what's been called, since then, the Lost Rune.
The other eight are known to Mages: Pirr that protects
from madness and from wind and fire, Ges that gives
endurance, and so on. But the broken rune was the one
that bound the lands. It was the Bond-Rune, the sign
of dominion, the sign of peace. No king could rule well
if he did not rule beneath that sign. No one knows how
it was written. Since it was lost there have been no
great kings in Havnor. There have been princes and
tyrants, and wars and quarreling among all the lands of
Earthsea.

"So the wise lords and Mages of the Archipelago
wanted the Ring of Erreth-Akbe, that they might re-
store the lost rune. But at last they gave up sending men
out to seek it, since none could take the one half from
the Tombs of Atuan, and the other half, which Erreth-
Akbe gave to a Kargish king, was lost long since. They
said there was no use in the search. That was many
hundred years ago.

"Now I come into it thus. When I was a little older
than you are now, I was on a . . . chase, a kind of hunt
across the sea. That which I hunted tricked me, so that
I was cast up on a desert isle, not far off the coasts of
Karego-At and Atuan, south and west of here. It was a
little islet, not much more than a sandbar, with long
grassy dunes down the middle, and a spring of salty
water, and nothing else.

"Yet two people lived there. An old man and
woman; brother and sister, I think. They were terrified
of me. They had not seen any other human face for—
how long? Years, tens of years. But I was in need, and
they were kind to me. They had a hut of driftwood,
and a fire. The old woman gave me food, mussels she
pulled from the rocks at low tide, dried meat of sea-
birds they killed by throwing stones. She was afraid of
me, but she gave me food. Then when I did nothing to
frighten her, she came to trust me, and she showed me

her treasure. She had a treasure, too. . . . It was a little dress. All of silk stuff, with pearls. A little child's dress, a princess' dress. She was wearing uncured sealskin.

"We couldn't talk. I didn't know the Kargish tongue then, and they knew no language of the Archipelago, and little enough of their own. They must have been brought there as young children, and left to die. I don't know why, and doubt that they knew. They knew nothing but the island, the wind, and the sea. But when I left she gave me a present. She gave me the lost half of the Ring of Erreth-Akbe."

He paused for a while.

"I didn't know it for what it was, no more than she did. The greatest gift of this age of the world, and it was given by a poor old foolish woman in sealskins to a silly lout who stuffed it into his pocket and said 'Thanks!' and sailed off. . . . Well, so I went on, and did what I had to do. And then other things came up, and I went to the Dragons' Run, westward, and so on. But all the time I kept the thing with me, because I felt a gratitude towards that old woman who had given me the only present she had to give. I put a chain through one of the holes pierced in it, and wore it, and never thought about it. And then one day on Selidor, the Farthest Isle, the land where Erreth-Akbe died in his battle with the dragon Orm—on Selidor I spoke with a dragon, one of that lineage of Orm. He told me what I wore upon my breast.

"He thought it very funny that I hadn't known. Dragons think we are amusing. But they remember Erreth-Akbe; him they speak of as if he were a dragon, not a man.

"When I came back to the Inmost Isles, I went at last to Havnor. I was born on Gont, which lies not far west of your Kargish lands, and I had wandered a good deal since, but I had never been to Havnor. It was time to go there. I saw the white towers, and spoke with the great men, the merchants and the princes and the lords of the ancient domains. I told them what I had. I told them that if they liked, I would go seek the rest of the ring in the Tombs of Atuan, in order to find the Lost Rune, the key to peace. For we need peace sorely in the world. They were full of praise; and one of them even gave me money to provision my boat. So I learned your tongue, and came to Atuan."

He fell silent, gazing before him into the shadows.

"Didn't the people in our towns know you for a Westerner, by your skin, by your speech?"

"Oh, it's easy to fool people," he said rather absently, "if you know the tricks. You make some illusion-changes, and nobody but another Mage will see through them. And you have no wizards or Mages here in the Kargish lands. That's a queer thing. You banished all your wizards long ago, and forbade the practice of the Art Magic; and now you scarcely believe in it."

"I was taught to disbelieve in it. It is contrary to the teachings of the Priest Kings. But I know that only sorcery could have got you to the Tombs, and in at the door of red rock."

"Not only sorcery, but good advice also. We use writing more than you, I think. Do you know how to read?"

"No. It is one of the black arts."

He nodded. "But a useful one," he said. "An ancient unsuccessful thief left certain descriptions of the Tombs of Atuan, and instructions for entering, if one were able to use one of the Great Spells of Opening. All this was written down in a book in the treasury of a prince of Havnor. He let me read it. So I got as far as the great cavern—"

"The Undertomb."

"The thief who wrote the way to enter thought that the treasure was there, in the Undertomb. So I looked there, but I had the feeling that it must be better hidden, farther on in the maze. I knew the entrance to the Labyrinth, and when I saw you, I went to it, thinking to hide in the maze and search it. That was a mistake, of course. The Nameless Ones had hold of me already, bewildering my mind. And since then I have grown only weaker and stupider. One must not submit to them, one must resist, keep one's spirit always strong and certain. I learned that a long time ago. But it's hard to do, here, where they are so strong. They are not gods, Tenar. But they are stronger than any man."

They were both silent for a long time.

"What else did you find in the treasure chests?" she asked dully.

"Rubbish. Gold, jewels, crowns, swords. Nothing to which any man alive has any claim.... Tell me this, Tenar. How were you chosen to be the Priestess of the Tombs?"

"When the First Priestess dies they go looking all through Atuan for a girl-baby born on the night the Priestess died. And they always find one. Because it is the Priestess reborn. When the child is five they bring it here to the Place. And when it is six it is given to the Dark Ones and its soul is eaten by them. And so it belongs to them, and has belonged to them since the beginning days. And it has no name."

"Do you believe that?"

"I have always believed it."

"Do you believe it now?"

She said nothing.

Again the shadowy silence fell between them. After a long time she said, "Tell me . . . tell me about the dragons in the West."

"Tenar, what will you do? We can't sit here telling each other tales until the candle burns out, and the darkness comes again."

"I don't know what to do. I am afraid." She sat erect on the stone chest, her hands clenched one in the other, and spoke loudly, like one in pain. She said, "I am afraid of the dark."

He answered softly. "You must make a choice. Either you must leave me, lock the door, go up to your altars and give me to your Masters; then go to the Priestess Kossil and make your peace with her—and that is the end of the story—or, you must unlock the door, and go out of it, with me. Leave the Tombs, leave Atuan, and come with me oversea. And that is the beginning of the story. You must be Arha, or you must be Tenar. You cannot be both."

The deep voice was gentle and certain. She looked through the shadows into his face, which was hard and scarred, but had in it no cruelty, no deceit.

"If I leave the service of the Dark Ones, they will kill me. If I leave this place I will die."

"You will not die. Arha will die."

"I cannot. . . ."

"To be reborn one must die, Tenar. It is not so hard as it looks from the other side."

"They would not let us get out. Ever."

"Perhaps not. Yet it's worth trying. You have knowledge, and I have skill, and between us we have. . . ." He paused.

"We have the Ring of Erreth-Akbe."

"Yes, that. But I thought also of another thing between us. Call it trust. . . . That is one of its names. It is a very great thing. Though each of us alone is weak, having that we are strong, stronger than the Powers of the Dark." His eyes were clear and bright in his scarred face. "Listen, Tenar!" he said. "I came here a thief, an enemy, armed against you; and you showed me mercy, and trusted me. And I have trusted you from the first time I saw your face, for one moment in the cave beneath the Tombs, beautiful in darkness. You have proved your trust in me. I have made no return. I will give you what I have to give. My true name is Ged. And this is yours to keep." He had risen, and he held out to her a semicircle of pierced and carven silver. "Let the ring be rejoined," he said.

She took it from his hand. She slipped from her neck the silver chain on which the other half was strung, and took it off the chain. She laid the two pieces in her palm so that the broken edges met, and it looked whole.

She did not raise her face.

"I will come with you," she said.

The Anger
of the Dark

When she said that, the man named Ged put his hand
over hers that held the broken talisman. She looked up
startled, and saw him flushed with life and triumph,
smiling. She was dismayed and frightened of him.
"You have set us both free," he said. "Alone, no one
wins freedom. Come, let's waste no time while we still
have time! Hold it out again, for a little." She had
closed her fingers over the pieces of silver, but at his re-
quest she held them out again on her hand, the broken
edges touching.

He did not take them, but put his fingers on them.
He said a couple of words, and sweat suddenly sprang
out on his face. She felt a queer little tremor on the
palm of her hand, as if a small animal sleeping there

had moved. Ged sighed; his tense stance relaxed, and he wiped his forehead.

"There," he said, and picking up the Ring of Erreth-Akbe he slid it over the fingers of her right hand, narrowly over the breadth of the hand, and up onto the wrist. "There!" and he regarded it with satisfaction. "It fits. It must be a woman's arm-ring, or a child's."

"Will it hold?' she murmured, nervously, feeling the strip of silver slip cold and delicate on her thin arm.

"It will. I couldn't put a mere mending charm on the Ring of Erreth-Akbe, like a village witch mending a kettle. I had to use a Patterning, and make it whole. It is whole now as if it had never been broken. Tenar, we must be gone. I'll bring the bag and flask. Wear your cloak. Is there anything more?"

As she fumbled at the door, unlocking it, he said, "I wish I had my staff," and she replied, still whispering, "It's just outside the door. I brought it."

"Why did you bring it?" he asked curiously.

"I thought of . . . taking you to the door. Letting you go."

"That was a choice you didn't have. You could keep me a slave, and be a slave; or set me free, and come free with me. Come, little one, take courage, turn the key."

She turned the dragon-hafted key and opened the door on the low, black corridor. She went out of the Treasury of the Tombs with the ring of Erreth-Akbe on her arm, and the man followed her.

There was a low vibration, not quite a noise, in the rock of the walls and floor and vaulting. It was like distant thunder, like something huge falling a great way off.

The hair on her head rose up, and without stopping to reason she blew out the candle in the tin lantern. She heard the man move behind her; his quiet voice said, so close that his breath stirred her hair, "Leave the lantern. I can make light if need be. What time is it, outside?"

"Long past midnight when I came here."

"We must go forward then."

But he did not move. She realized that she must lead him. Only she knew the way out of the Labyrinth, and he waited to follow her. She set out, stooping because the tunnel here was so low, but keeping a pretty good pace. From unseen cross-passages came a cold breath and a sharp, dank odor, the lifeless smell of the huge hollowness beneath them. When the passage grew a little higher and she could stand upright, she went slower, counting her steps as they approached the pit. Light-footed, aware of all her movements, he followed a short way behind her. The instant she stopped, he stopped.

"Here's the pit," she whispered. "I can't find the ledge. No, here. Be careful, I think the stones are coming loose. . . . No, no, wait—it's loose—" She sidled back to safety as the stones teetered under her feet. The man caught her arm and held her. Her heart pounded. "The ledge isn't safe, the stones are coming loose."

"I'll make a little light, and look at them. Maybe I can mend them with the right word. It's all right, little one."

She thought how strange it was that he called her what Manan had always called her. And as he kindled a faint glow on the end of his staff, like the glow on rotting wood or a star behind fog, and stepped out onto the narrow way beside the black abyss, she saw the bulk looming in the farther dark beyond him, and knew it for Manan. But her voice was caught in her throat as in a noose, and she could not cry out.

As Manan reached out to push him off his shaky perch into the pit beside him, Ged looked up, saw him, and with a shout of surprise or rage struck out at him with the staff. At the shout the light blazed up white and intolerable, straight in the eunuch's face. Manan flung up one of his big hands to shield his eyes, lunged desperately to catch hold of Ged, and missed, and fell.

He made no cry as he fell. No sound came up out of the black pit, no sound of his body hitting the bottom, no sound of his death, none at all. Clinging perilously to the ledge, kneeling frozen at the lip, Ged and Tenar did not move; listened; heard nothing.

The light was gray wisp, barely visible.

"Come!" Ged said, holding out his hand; she took it, and in three bold steps he brought her across. He quenched the light. She went ahead of him again to lead the way. She was quite numb and did not think of anything. Only after some time she thought, *Is it right or left?*

She stopped.

Halted a few steps behind her, he said softly, "What is it?"

"I am lost. Make the light."

"Lost?"

"I have . . . I have lost count of the turnings."

"I kept count," he said, coming a little closer. "A left turn after the pit; then a right, and a right again."

"Then the next will be right again," she said automatically, but she did not move. "Make the light."

"The light won't show us the way, Tenar."

"Nothing will. It is lost. We are lost."

The dead silence closed in upon her whisper, ate it.

She felt the movement and warmth of the other, close to her in the cold dark. He sought her hand and took it. "Go on, Tenar. The next turn to the right."

"Make a light," she pleaded. "The tunnels twist so. . . ."

"I cannot. I have no strength to spare. Tenar, they are— They know that we left the Treasury. They know that we're past the pit. They are seeking us, seeking our will, our spirit. To quench it, to devour it. I must keep that alight. All my strength is going into that. I must withstand them; with you. With your help. We must go on."

"There is no way out," she said, but she took one step forward. Then she took another, hesitant as if beneath each step the black hollow void gaped open, the emptiness under the earth. The warm, hard grip of his hand was on her hand. They went forward.

After what seemed a long time they came to the flight of steps. It had not seemed so steep before, the steps hardly more than slimy notches in the rock. But they climbed it, and then went on a little more rapidly, for she knew that the curving passage went a long way without side turnings after the steps. Her fingers, trailing the left-hand wall for guidance, crossed a gap, an opening to the left. "Here," she murmured; but he seemed to hold back, as if something in her movements made him doubtful.

"No," she muttered in confusion, "not this, it's the next turn to the left. I don't know. I can't do it. There's no way out."

"We are going to the Painted Room," the quiet voice said in the darkness. "How should we go there?"

"The left turn after this."

She led on. They made the long circuit, past two false leads, to the passage that branched rightwards towards the Painted Room.

"Straight on," she whispered, and now the long unraveling of the darkness went better, for she knew these passages towards the iron door and had counted their turns a hundred times; the strange weight that lay upon her mind could not confuse her about them, if she did not try to think. But all the time they were getting nearer and nearer to that which weighed upon her and pressed against her; and her legs were so tired and heavy that she whimpered once or twice with the labor of making them move. And beside her the man would breathe deep, and hold the breath, again and again, like one making a mighty effort with all the strength of his body. Sometimes his voice broke out, hushed and sharp, in a word or fragment of a word. So they came at last to the iron door; and in sudden terror she put out her hand.

The door was open.

"Quick!" she said, and pulled her companion through. Then, on the further side, she halted.

"Why was it open?" she said.

"Because your Masters need your hands to shut it for them."

"We are coming to. . . ." Her voice failed her.

"To the center of the darkness. I know. Yet we're out of the Labyrinth. What ways out of the Undertomb are there?"

"Only one. The door you entered doesn't open from

within. The way goes through the cavern and up passages to a trapdoor in a room behind the Throne. In the Hall of the Throne."

"Then we must go that way."

"But she is there," the girl whispered. "There in the Undertomb. In the cavern. Digging in the empty grave. I cannot pass her, oh, I cannot pass her again!"

"She will have gone by now."

"I cannot go there."

"Tenar, I hold the roof up over our heads, this moment. I keep the walls from closing in upon us. I keep the ground from opening beneath our feet. I have done this since we passed the pit where their servant waited. If I can hold off the earthquake, do you fear to meet one human soul with me? Trust me, as I have trusted you! Come with me now."

They went forward.

The endless tunnel opened out. The sense of a greater air met them, an enlarging of the dark. They had entered the great cave beneath the Tombstones.

They started to circle it, keeping to the right-hand wall. Tenar had gone only a few steps when she paused. "What is it?" she murmured, her voice barely passing her lips. There was a noise in the dead, vast, black bubble of air: a tremor or shaking, a sound heard by the blood and felt in the bones. The time-carven walls beneath her fingers thrummed, thrummed.

"Go forward," the man's voice said, dry and strained. "Hurry, Tenar."

As she stumbled forward she cried out in her mind, which was as dark, as shaken as the subterranean vault, "Forgive me. O my Masters, O unnamed ones, most ancient ones, forgive me, forgive me!"

There was no answer. There had never been an answer.

They came to the passage beneath the Hall, climbed the stairs, came to the last steps up and the trapdoor at their head. It was shut, as she always left it. She pressed the spring that opened it. It did not open.

"It is broken," she said. "It is locked."

He came up past her and put his back against the trap. It did not move.

"It's not locked, but held down by something heavy."

"Can you open it?"

"Perhaps. I think she'll be waiting there. Has she men with her?"

"Duby and Uahto, maybe other wardens—men cannot come there—"

"I can't make a spell of opening, and hold off the people waiting up there, and withstand the will of the darkness, all at one time," said his steady voice, considering. "We must try the other door then, the door in the rocks, by which I came in. She knows that it can't be opened from within?"

"She knows. She let me try it once."

"Then she may discount it. Come. Come, Tenar!"

She had sunk down on the stone steps, which hummed and shivered as if a great bowstring were being plucked in the depths beneath them.

"What is it—the shaking?"

"Come," he said, so steady and certain that she obeyed, and crept back down the passages and stairs, back to the dreadful cavern.

At the entrance so great a weight of blind and dire hatred came pressing down upon her, like the weight of the earth itself, that she cowered and without knowing it cried out aloud, "They are here! They are here!"

"Then let them know that we are here," the man said, and from his staff and hands leapt forth a white radiance that broke as a sea-wave breaks in sunlight, against the thousand diamonds of the roof and walls: a glory of light, through which the two fled, straight across the great cavern, their shadows racing from them into the white traceries and the glittering crevices and the empty, open grave. To the low doorway they ran, down the tunnel, stooping over, she first, he following. There in the tunnel the rocks boomed, and moved under their feet. Yet the light was with them still, dazzling. As she saw the dead rock-face before her, she heard over the thundering of the earth his voice speak-

ing one word, and as she fell to her knees his staff
struck down, over her head, against the red rock of the
shut door. The rocks burned white as if afire, and burst
asunder.

Outside them was the sky, paling to dawn. A few
white stars lay high and cool within it.

Tenar saw the stars and felt the sweet wind on her
face; but she did not get up. She crouched on hands
and knees there between the earth and sky.

The man, a strange dark figure in that half-light before the dawn, turned and pulled at her arm to make
her get up. His face was black and twisted like a
demon's. She cowered away from him, shrieking in a
thick voice not her own, as if a dead tongue moved in
her mouth, "No! No! Don't touch me—leave me—
Go!" And she writhed back away from him, into the
crumbling, lipless mouth of the Tombs.

His hard grip loosened. He said in a quiet voice, "By
the bond you wear I bid you come, Tenar."

She saw the starlight on the silver of the ring on her
arm. Her eyes on that, she rose, staggering. She put her
hand in his, and came with him. She could not run.
They walked down the hill. From the black mouth
among the rocks behind them issued forth a long, long,
groaning howl of hatred and lament. Stones fell about
them. The ground quivered. They went on, she with
her eyes still fixed on the glimmer of starlight on her
wrist.

They were in the dim valley westward of the Place.
Now they began to climb; and all at once he bade her
turn. "See—"

She turned, and saw. They were across the valley, on
a level now with the Tombstones, the nine great mono-
liths that stood or lay above the cavern of diamonds and
graves. The stones that stood were moving. They jerked,
and leaned slowly like the masts of ships. One of
them seemed to twitch and rise taller; then a shudder
went through it, and it fell. Another fell, smashing
crossways on the first. Behind them the low dome of
the Hall of the Throne, black against the yellow light in
the east, quivered. The walls bulged. The whole great

ruinous mass of stone and masonry changed shape like clay in running water, sank in upon itself, and with a roar and sudden storm of splinters and dust slid sideways and collapsed. The earth of the valley rippled and bucked; a kind of wave ran up the hillside, and a huge crack opened among the Tombstones, gaping on the blackness underneath, oozing dust like gray smoke. The stones that still stood upright toppled into it and were swallowed. Then with a crash that seemed to echo off the sky itself, the raw black lips of the crack closed together; and the hills shook once, and grew still.

She looked from the horror of earthquake to the man beside her, whose face she had never seen by daylight. "You held it back," she said, and her voice piped like the wind in a reed, after that mighty bellowing and crying of the earth. "You held back the earthquake, the anger of the dark."

"We must go on," he said, turning away from the sunrise and the ruined Tombs. "I am tired, I am cold. . . ." He stumbled as they went, and she took his arm. Neither could go faster than a dragging walk. Slowly, like two tiny spiders on a great wall, they toiled up the immense slope of the hill, until at the top they stood on dry ground yellowed by the rising sun and streaked with the long, sparse shadows of the sage. Before them the western mountains stood, their feet purple, their upper slopes gold. The two paused a moment, then passed over the crest of the hill, out of sight of the Place of the Tombs, and were gone.

The Western
Mountains

Tenar woke, struggling up from bad dreams, out of places where she had walked so long that all the flesh had fallen from her and she could see the double white bones of her arms glimmer faintly in the dark. She opened her eyes to a golden light, and smelled the pungency of sage. A sweetness came into her as she woke, a pleasure that filled her slowly and wholly till it overflowed, and she sat up, stretching her arms out from the black sleeves of her robe, and looked about her in unquestioning delight.

It was evening. The sun was down behind the mountains that loomed close and high to westward, but its afterglow filled all earth and sky: a vast, clear, wintry sky, a vast, barren, golden land of mountains and wide valleys. The wind was down. It was cold, and absolutely silent. Nothing moved. The leaves of the sagebushes nearby were dry and gray, the stalks of tiny dried-up desert herbs prickled her hand. The huge silent glory of light burned on every twig and withered leaf and stem, on the hills, in the air.

She looked to her left and saw the man lying on the desert ground, his cloak pulled round him, one arm under his head, fast asleep. His face in sleep was stern, almost frowning; but his left hand lay relaxed on the dirt, beside a small thistle that still bore its ragged cloak of gray fluff and its tiny defense of spikes and spines. The man and the small desert thistle; the thistle and the sleeping man. . . .

He was one whose power was akin to, and as strong as, the Old Powers of the earth; one who talked with dragons, and held off earthquakes with his word. And there he lay asleep on the dirt, with a little thistle growing by his hand. It was very strange. Living, being in the world, was a much greater and stranger thing than she had ever dreamed. The glory of the sky touched his dusty hair, and turned the thistle gold for a little while.

The light was slowly fading. As it did so, the cold seemed to grow intenser minute by minute. Tenar got up and began to gather dry sagebrush, picking up fallen twigs, breaking off the tough branches that grew as gnarled and massive, in their scale, as the limbs of oaks. They had stopped here about noon, when it was warm, and they could go no farther for weariness. A couple of stunted junipers, and the westward slope of the ridge they had just descended, had offered shelter enough; they had drunk a little water from the flask, and lain down, and gone to sleep.

There was a litter of larger branches under the little trees, which she gathered. Scooping out a pit in an angle of earth-embedded rocks, she built up a fire, and lit it with her flint and steel. The tinder of sage leaves and twigs caught at once. Dry branches bloomed into rosy flame, scented with resin. Now it seemed quite dark, all around the fire; and the stars were coming out again in the tremendous sky.

The snap and crack of the flames roused the sleeper. He sat up, rubbing his hands over his grimy face, and at last got up stiffly and came close to the fire.

"I wonder—" he said sleepily.

"I know, but we can't last the night here without a fire. It gets too cold." After a minute she added, "Unless you have some magic that would keep us warm, or that would hide the fire. . . ."

He sat down by the fire, his feet almost in it, his arms round his knees. "Brr," he said. "A fire is much better than magic. I've put a little illusion about us here; if someone comes by, we might look like sticks and stones to him. What do you think? Will they be following us?"

"I fear it, yet I don't think they will. No one but Kossil knew of your being there. Kossil, and Manan. And they are dead. Surely she was in the Hall when it fell. She was waiting at the trapdoor. And the others, the rest, they must think that I was in the Hall or the Tombs, and was crushed in the earthquake." She too put her arms round her knees, and shuddered. "I hope the other buildings didn't fall. It was hard to see from the hill, there was so much dust. Surely all the temples and houses didn't fall, the Big House where all the girls sleep."

"I think not. It was the Tombs that devoured themselves. I saw a gold roof of some temple as we turned away; it still stood. And there were figures down the hill, people running."

"What will they say, what will they think. . . . Poor Penthe! She might have to become the High Priestess of the Godking now. And it was always she who wanted to run away. Not I. Maybe now she'll run away." Tenar smiled. There was a joy in her that no thought nor dread could darken, that same sure joy that had risen in her, waking in the golden light. She opened her bag and took out two small, flat loaves; she handed one across the fire to Ged, and bit into the other. The bread was tough, and sour, and very good to eat.

They munched together in silence awhile.

"How far are we from the sea?"

"It took me two nights and two days coming. It'll take us longer going."

"I'm strong," she said.

"You are. And valiant. But your companion's tired," he said with a smile. "And we haven't any too much bread."

"Will we find water?"

"Tomorrow, in the mountains."

"Can you find food for us?" she asked, rather vaguely and timidly.

"Hunting takes time, and weapons."

"I meant, with, you know, spells."

"I can call a rabbit," he said, poking the fire with a twisted stick of juniper. "The rabbits are coming out of their holes all around us, now. Evening's their time. I could call one by name, and he'd come. But would you catch and skin and broil a rabbit that you'd called to you thus? Perhaps if you were starving. But it would be a breaking of trust, I think."

"Yes. I thought, perhaps you could just . . ."

"Summon up a supper," he said. "Oh, I could. On golden plates, if you like. But that's illusion, and when you eat illusions you end up hungrier than before. It's about as nourishing as eating your own words." She saw his white teeth flash a moment in the firelight.

"Your magic is peculiar," she said, with a little dignity of equals, Priestess addressing Mage. "It appears to be useful only for large matters."

He laid more wood on the fire, and it flared up in a juniper-scented fireworks of sparks and crackles.

"Can you really call a rabbit?" Tenar inquired suddenly.

"Do you want me to?"

She nodded.

He turned away from the fire and said softly into the immense and starlit dark, "*Kebbo . . . O kebbo . . .*"

Silence. No sound. No motion. Only presently, at the very edge of the flickering firelight, a round eye like a pebble of jet, very near the ground. A curve of furry back; an ear, long, alert, upraised.

Ged spoke again. The ear flicked, gained a sudden partner-ear out of the shadow; then as the little beast turned Tenar saw it entire for an instant, the small, soft, lithe hop of it returning unconcerned to its business in the night.

"Ah!' she said, letting out her breath. "That's lovely." Presently she asked, "Could I do that?"

"Well—"

"It is a secret," she said at once, dignified again.

"The rabbit's *name* is a secret. At least, one should not use it lightly, for no reason. But what is not a secret, but rather a gift, or a mystery, do you see, is the power of calling."

"Oh," she said, "that you have. I know!" There was a passion in her voice, not hidden by pretended mockery. He looked at her and did not answer.

He was indeed still worn out by his struggle against the Nameless Ones; he had spent his strength in the quaking tunnels. Though he had won, he had little spirit left for exultation. He soon curled up again, as near the fire as he could get, and slept.

Tenar sat feeding the fire and watching the blaze of the winter constellations from horizon to horizon until her head grew giddy with splendor and silence, and she dozed off.

They both woke. The fire was dead. The stars she had watched were now far over the mountains and new ones had risen in the east. It was the cold that woke them, the dry cold of the desert night, the wind like a knife of ice. A veil of cloud was coming over the sky from the southwest.

The gathered firewood was almost gone. "Let's walk," Ged said, "it's not long till dawn." His teeth chattered so that she could hardly understand him. They set out, climbing the long slow slope westward. The bushes and rocks showed black in starlight, and it was as easy to walk as in the day. After a cold first while, the walking warmed them; they stopped crouching and shivering, and began to go easier. So by sunrise they were on the first rise of the western mountains, which had walled in Tenar's life till then.

They stopped in a grove of trees whose golden, quivering leaves still clung to the boughs. He told her they were aspens; she knew no trees but juniper, and the sickly poplars by the river-springs, and the forty apple trees of the orchard of the Place. A small bird among the aspens said "dee, dee," in a small voice. Under the trees ran a stream, narrow but powerful, shouting, muscular over its rocks and falls, too hasty to freeze. Tenar was almost afraid of it. She was used to the desert where things are silent and move slowly: sluggish rivers, shadows of clouds, vultures circling.

They divided a piece of bread and a last crumbling bit of cheese for breakfast, rested a little, and went on.

By evening they were up high. It was overcast and windy, freezing weather. They camped in the valley of another stream, where there was plenty of wood, and this time built up a sturdy fire of logs by which they could keep fairly warm.

Tenar was happy. She had found a squirrel's cache of nuts, exposed by the falling of a hollow tree: a couple of pounds of fine walnuts and a smooth-shelled kind that Ged, not knowing the Kargish name, called *ubir*. She cracked them one by one between a flat stone and a hammerstone, and handed every second nutmeat to the man.

"I wish we could stay here," she said, looking down at the windy, twilit valley between the hills. "I like this place."

"This is a good place," he agreed.

"People would never come here."

"Not often. . . . I was born in the mountains," he said, "on the Mountain of Gont. We shall pass it, sailing to Havnor, if we take the northern way. It's beautiful to see it in winter, rising all white out of the sea, like a greater wave. My village was by just such a stream as this one. Where were you born, Tenar?"

"In the north of Atuan, in Entat, I think. I can't remember it."

"They took you so young?"

"I was five. I remember a fire on a hearth, and ... nothing else."

He rubbed his jaw, which though it had acquired a sparse beard, was at least clean; despite the cold, both of them had washed in the mountain streams. He rubbed his jaw and looked thoughtful and severe. She watched him, and never could she have said what was in her heart as she watched him, in the firelight, in the mountain dusk.

"What are you going to do in Havnor?" he said, asking the question of the fire, not of her. "You are—more than I had realized—truly reborn."

She nodded, smiling a little. She felt newborn.

"You should learn the language, at least."

"Your language?"

"Yes."

"I'd like to."

"Well, then. This is *kabat*," and he tossed a little stone into the lap of her black robe.

"Kabat. Is that in the dragon-tongue?"

"No, no. You don't want to work spells, you want to talk with other men and women!"

"But what is a pebble in the dragon's tongue?"

"*Tolk*," he said. "But I am not making you my apprentice sorcerer. I'm teaching you the language people speak in the Archipelago, the Inner Lands. I had to learn your language before I came here."

"You speak it oddly."

"No doubt. Now, *arkemmi kabat*," and he held out his hands for her to give him the pebble.

"Must I go to Havnor?" she said.

"Where else would you go, Tenar?"

She hesitated.

"Havnor is a beautiful city," he said. "And you bring it the ring, the sign of peace, the lost treasure. They'll welcome you in Havnor as a princess. They'll do you honor for the great gift you bring them, and bid you welcome, and make you welcome. They are a noble and generous people in that city. They'll call you the White Lady because of your fair skin, and they'll love you the more because you are so young. And because you are beautiful. You'll have a hundred dresses like the one I showed you by illusion, but real ones. You'll meet with praise, and gratitude, and love. You who have known nothing but solitude and envy and the dark."

"There was Manan," she said, defensive, her mouth trembling just a little. "He loved me and was kind to me, always. He protected me as well as he knew how, and I killed him for it; he fell into the black pit. I don't want to go to Havnor. I don't want to go there. I want to stay here."

"Here—in Atuan?"

"In the mountains. Where we are now."

"Tenar," he said in his grave, quiet voice, "we'll stay then. I haven't my knife, and if it snows it will be hard. But so long as we can find food—"

"No. I know we can't stay. I'm merely being foolish," Tenar said, and got up, scattering walnut shells, to lay new wood on the fire. She stood thin and very straight in her torn, dirt-stained gown and cloak of black. "All I know is of no use now," she said, "and I haven't learned anything else. I will try to learn."

Ged looked away, wincing as if in pain.

Next day they crossed the summit of the tawny range. In the pass a hard wind blew, with snow in it, stinging and blinding. It was not until they had come down a long way on the other side, out from under the snow clouds of the peaks, that Tenar saw the land beyond the mountain wall. It was all green—green of pines, of grasslands, of sown fields and fallows. Even in the dead of winter, when the thickets were bare and the forests full of gray boughs, it was a green land, humble and mild. They looked down on it from a high, rocky slant of the mountainside. Wordless, Ged pointed to the west, where the sun was getting low behind a thick cream and roil of clouds. The sun itself was hidden, but there was a glitter on the horizon, almost like the dazzle of the crystal walls of the Undertomb, a kind of joyous shimmering off on the edge of the world.

"What is that?" the girl said, and he: "The sea."

Shortly afterward, she saw a less wonderful thing than that, but wonderful enough. They came on a road, and followed it; and it brought them by dusk into a village: ten or a dozen houses strung along the road. She looked at her companion in alarm when she realized they were coming among men. She looked, and did not see him. Beside her, in Ged's clothing, and with his gait, and in his shoes, strode another man. He had a white skin, and no beard. He glanced at her; his eyes were blue. He winked.

"Will I fool 'em?" he said. "How are your clothes?"

She looked down at herself. She had on a country-woman's brown skirt and jacket, and a large red woolen shawl.

"Oh," she said, stopping short. "Oh, you are—you *are* Ged!" As she said his name she saw him perfectly clearly, the dark, scarred face she knew, the dark eyes; yet there stood the milk-faced stranger.

"Don't say my true name before others. Nor will I say yours. We are brother and sister, come from Tenacbah. And I think I'll ask for a bite of supper if I see a kindly face." He took her hand and they entered the village.

They left it next morning with full stomachs, after a pleasant sleep in a hayloft.

"Do Mages often beg?" asked Tenar, on the road between green fields, where goats and little spotted cattle grazed.

"Why do you ask?"

"You seemed used to begging. In fact you were good at it."

"Well, yes. I've begged all my life, if you look at it that way. Wizards don't own much, you know. In fact nothing but their staff and clothing, if they wander. They are received and given food and shelter, by most people, gladly. They do make some return."

"What return?"

"Well, that woman in the village. I cured her goats."

"What was wrong with them?"

"They both had infected udders. I used to herd goats when I was a boy."

"Did you tell her you'd cured them?"

"No. How could I? Why should I?"

After a pause she said, "I see your magic is not good only for large things."

"Hospitality," he said, "kindness to a stranger, that's a very large thing. Thanks are enough, of course. But I was sorry for the goats."

In the afternoon they came by a large town. It was built of clay brick, and walled round in the Kargish fashion, with overhanging battlements, watchtowers at the four corners, and a single gate, under which drovers were herding a big flock of sheep. The red tile roofs of a hundred or more houses poked up over the walls of yellowish brick. At the gate stood two guards in the red-plumed helmets of the Godking's service. Tenar had seen men in such helmets come, once a year or so, to the Place, escorting offerings of slaves or money to the Godking's temple. When she told Ged that, as they passed by outside the walls, he said, "I saw them too, as a boy. They came raiding to Gont. They came into my village, to plunder it. But they were driven off. And there was a battle down by Armouth, on the shore; many men were killed, hundreds, they say. Well, perhaps now that the ring is rejoined and the Lost Rune remade, there will be no more such raiding and killing between the Kargish Empire and the Inner Lands."

"It would be foolish if such things went on," said Tenar. "What would the Godking ever do with so many slaves?"

Her companion appeared to ponder this awhile. "If the Kargish lands defeated the Archipelago, you mean?"

She nodded.

"I don't think that would be likely to happen."

"But look how strong the Empire is—that great city, with its walls, and all its men. How could your lands stand against them, if they attacked?"

"That is not a very big city," he said cautiously and gently. "I too would have thought it tremendous, when I was new from my mountain. But there are many, many cities in Earthsea, among which this is only a town. There are many, many lands. You will see them, Tenar."

She said nothing. She trudged along the road, her face set.

"It is marvelous to see them: the new lands rising from the sea as your boat comes towards them. The farmlands and forests, the cities with their harbors and palaces, the marketplaces where they sell everything in the world."

She nodded. She knew he was trying to hearten her, but she had left joy up in the mountains, in the twilit valley of the stream. There was a dread in her now that grew and grew. All that lay ahead of her was unknown. She knew nothing but the desert and the Tombs. What good was that? She knew the turnings of a ruined maze, she knew the dances danced before a fallen altar. She knew nothing of forests, or cities, or the hearts of men.

She said suddenly, "Will you stay with me there?"

She did not look at him. He was in his illusory disguise, a white-skinned Kargish countryman, and she did not like to see him so. But his voice was unchanged, the same voice that had spoken in the darkness of the Labyrinth.

He was slow to answer. "Tenar, I go where I am sent. I follow my calling. It has not yet let me stay in any land for long. Do you see that? I do what I must do. Where I go, I must go alone. So long as you need me, I'll be with you in Havnor. And if you ever need me again, call me. I will come. I would come from my grave if you called me, Tenar! But I cannot stay with you."

She said nothing. After a while he said, "You will not need me long, there. You will be happy."

She nodded, accepting, silent.

They went on side by side towards the sea.

Voyage

He had hidden his boat in a cave on the side of a great rocky headland, Cloud Cape it was called by the villagers nearby, one of whom gave them a bowl of fish stew for their supper. They made their way down the cliffs to the beach in the last light of the gray day. The cave was a narrow crack that went back into the rock for about thirty feet; its sandy floor was damp, for it lay just above the high-tide mark. Its opening was visible from sea, and Ged said they should not light a fire lest the night-fishermen out in their small craft along shore should see it and be curious. So they lay miserably on the sand, which seemed so soft between the fingers and was rock-hard to the tired body. And Tenar listened to the sea, a few yards below the cave mouth, crashing and sucking and booming on the rocks, and the thunder of it down the beach eastward for miles. Over and over

137

and over it made the same sounds, yet never quite the
same. It never rested. On all the shores of all the lands
in all the world, it heaved itself in these unresting waves,
and never ceased, and never was still. The desert, the
mountains: they stood still. They did not cry out forever
in a great, dull voice. The sea spoke forever, but its
language was foreign to her. She did not understand.

In the first gray light, when the tide was low, she
roused from uneasy sleep and saw the wizard go out of
the cave. She watched him walk, barefoot and with
belted cloak, on the black-haired rocks below, seeking
something. He came back, darkening the cave as he
entered. "Here," he said, holding out a handful of wet,
hideous things like purple rocks and orange lips.

"What are they?"

"Mussels, off the rocks. And those two are oysters,
even better. Look—like this." With the little dagger
from her keyring, which she had lent him up in the
mountains, he opened a shell and ate the orange mussel
with seawater as its sauce.

"You don't even cook it? You ate it alive!"

She would not look at him while he, shamefaced but
undeterred, went on opening and eating the shellfish
one by one.

When he was done, he went back into the cave to the
boat, which lay prow forward, kept from the sand by
several long driftwood logs. Tenar had looked at the
boat the night before, mistrustfully and without compre-
hension. It was much larger than she had thought boats
were, three times her own length. It was full of objects
she did not know the use of, and it looked dangerous.
On either side of its nose (which is what she called the
prow) an eye was painted; and in her halfsleep she had
constantly felt the boat staring at her.

Ged rummaged about inside it a moment and came
back with something: a packet of hard bread, well
wrapped to keep dry. He offered her a large piece.

"I'm not hungry."

He looked into her sullen face.

He put the bread away, wrapping it as before, and

then sat down in the mouth of the cave. "About two hours till the tide's back in," he said. "Then we can go. You had a restless night, why don't you sleep now."

"I'm not sleepy."

He made no answer. He sat there, in profile to her, cross-legged in the dark arch of rocks; the shining heave and movement of the sea was beyond him as she watched him from deeper in the cave. He did not move. He was still as the rocks themselves. Stillness spread out from him, like rings from a stone dropped in water. His silence became not absence of speech, but a thing in itself, like the silence of the desert.

After a long time Tenar got up and came to the mouth of the cave. He did not move. She looked down at his face. It was as if cast in copper—rigid, the dark eyes not shut, but looking down, the mouth serene.

He was as far beyond her as the sea.

Where was he now, on what way of the spirit did he walk? She could never follow him.

He had made her follow him. He had called her by her name, and she had come crouching to his hand, as the little wild desert rabbit had come to him out of the dark. And now that he had the ring, now that the Tombs were in ruin and their priestess forsworn forever, now he didn't need her, and went away where she could not follow. He would not stay with her. He had fooled her, and would leave her desolate.

She reached down and with one swift gesture plucked from his belt the little steel dagger she had given him. He moved no more than a robbed statue.

The dagger blade was only four inches long, sharp on one side; it was the miniature of a sacrificial knife. It was part of the garments of the Priestess of the Tombs, who must wear it along with the ring of keys, and a belt of horsehair, and other items some of which had no known purpose. She had never used the dagger for anything, except that in one of the dances performed at dark of the moon she would throw and catch it before the Throne. She had liked that dance; it was a wild one, with no music but the drumming of her own feet. She had used to cut her fingers, practicing it, till she got the trick of catching the knife handle every time. The little blade was sharp enough to cut a finger to the bone, or to cut the arteries of a throat. She would serve her Masters still, though they had betrayed her and forsaken her. They would guide and drive her hand in the last act of darkness. They would accept the sacrifice.

She turned upon the man, the knife held back in her right hand behind her hip. As she did so he raised his face slowly and looked at her. He had the look of one come from a long way off, one who has seen terrible things. His face was calm but full of pain. As he gazed up at her and seemed to see her more and more clearly, his expression cleared. At last he said, "Tenar," as if in greeting, and reached up his hand to touch the band of pierced and carven silver on her wrist. He did this as if reassuring himself, trustingly. He did not pay attention to the dagger in her hand. He looked away, at the waves, which heaved deep over the rocks below, and said with effort, "It's time. . . . Time we were going."

At the sound of his voice the fury left her. She was afraid.

"You'll leave them behind, Tenar. You're going free now," he said, getting up with sudden vigor. He stretched, and belted his cloak tight again. "Give me a hand with the boat. She's up on logs, for rollers. That's it, push . . . again. There, there, enough. Now be ready to hop in when I say 'hop.' This is a tricky place to launch from—once more. There! In you go!"—and leaping in after her, he caught her as she overbalanced, sat her down in the bottom of the boat, braced his legs wide, and standing to the oars sent the boat shooting out on an ebb wave over the rocks, out past the roaring foam-drenched head of the cape, and so to sea.

He shipped the oars when they were well away from shoal water, and stepped the mast. The boat looked very small, now that she was inside it and the sea was outside it.

He put up the sail. All the gear had a look of long, hard use, though the dull red sail was patched with great care and the boat was as clean and trim as could be. They were like their master: they had gone far, and had not been treated gently.

"Now," he said, "now we're away, now we're clear, we're clean gone, Tenar. Do you feel it?"

She did feel it. A dark hand had let go its lifelong hold upon her heart. But she did not feel joy, as she had in the mountains. She put her head down in her arms and cried, and her cheeks were salt and wet. She cried for the waste of her years in bondage to a useless evil. She wept in pain, because she was free.

What she had begun to learn was the weight of liberty. Freedom is a heavy load, a great and strange burden for the spirit to undertake. It is not easy. It is not a gift given, but a choice made, and the choice may be a hard one. The road goes upward towards the light; but the laden traveler may never reach the end of it.

Ged let her cry, and said no word of comfort; nor when she was done with tears and sat looking back towards the low blue land of Atuan, did he speak. His face was stern and alert, as if he were alone; he saw to the sail and the steering, quick and silent, looking always ahead.

In the afternoon he pointed rightward of the sun, towards which they now sailed. "That is Karego-At," he said, and Tenar following his gesture saw the distant loom of hills like clouds, the great island of the Godking. Atuan was out of sight behind them. Her heart was very heavy. The sun beat in her eyes like a hammer of gold.

Supper was dry bread, and dried smoked fish, which tasted vile to Tenar, and water from the boat's cask, which Ged had filled at a stream on Cloud Cape beach the evening before. The winter night came down soon and cold upon the sea. Far off to northward they saw for a while the tiny glitter of lights, yellow firelight in distant villages on the shore of Karego-At. These vanished in a haze that rose up from the ocean, and they were alone in the starless night over deep water.

She had curled up in the stern; Ged lay down in the prow, with the water cask for a pillow. The boat moved on steadily, the low swells slapping her sides a little, though the wind was only a faint breath from the south. Out here, away from the rocky shores, the sea too was silent; only as it touched the boat did it whisper a little.

"If the wind is from the south," Tenar said, whispering because the sea did, "doesn't the boat sail north?"

"Yes, unless we tack. But I've put the mage-wind in her sail, to the west. By tomorrow morning we should be out of Kargish waters. Then I'll let her go by the world's wind."

"Does it steer itself?"

"Yes," Ged replied with gravity, "given the proper instructions. She doesn't need many. She's been in the open sea, beyond the farthest isle of the East Reach; she's been to Selidor where Erreth-Akbe died, in the farthest West. She's a wise crafty boat, my *Lookfar*. You can trust her."

In the boat moved by magic over the great deep, the girl lay looking up into the dark. All her life she had looked into the dark; but this was a vaster darkness, this night on the ocean. There was no end to it. There was no roof. It went on out beyond the stars. No earthly Powers moved it. It had been before light, and would be after. It had been before life, and would be after. It went on beyond evil.

In the dark, she spoke: "The little island, where the talisman was given you, is that in this sea?"

"Yes," his voice answered out of the dark. "Somewhere. To the south, perhaps. I could not find it again."

"I know who she was, the old woman who gave you the ring."

"You know?"

"I was told the tale. It is part of the knowledge of the First Priestess. Thar told it to me, first when Kossil was there, then more fully when we were alone; it was the last time she talked to me before she died. There was a noble house in Hupun who fought against the rise of the High Priests in Awabath. The founder of the house was King Thoreg, and among the treasures he left his descendants was the half-ring, which Erreth-Akbe had given him."

"That indeed is told in the *Deed of Erreth-Akbe*. It says . . . in your tongue it says, 'When the ring was broken, half remained in the hand of the High Priest Intathin, and half in the hero's hand. And the High Priest sent the broken half to the Nameless, to the Ancient of the Earth in Atuan, and it went into the dark, into the lost places. But Erreth-Akbe gave the broken half into the hands of the maiden Tiarath, daughter of the wise king, saying: "Let it remain in the light, in the maiden's dowry, let it remain in this land until it be rejoined." So spoke the hero before he sailed to the west.' "

"So it must have gone from daughter to daughter of that house, over all the years. It was not lost, as your people thought. But as the High Priests made themselves into the Priest-Kings, and then when the Priest-Kings made the Empire and began to call themselves Godkings, all this time the house of Thoreg grew poorer and weaker. And at last, so Thar told me, there were only two of the lineage of Thoreg left, little children, a boy and a girl. The Godking in Awabath then was the father of him who rules now. He had the children stolen from their palace in Hupun. There was a prophecy that one of the descendants of Thoreg of Hupun would bring about the fall of the Empire in the end, and that frightened him. He had the children stolen away, and taken to a lonely isle somewhere out in the middle of the sea, and left there with nothing but the clothes they wore and a little food. He feared to kill them by knife or strangling or poison; they were of kingly blood, and murder of kings brings a curse even on the gods. They were named Ensar and Anthil. It was Anthil who gave you the broken ring."

He was silent a long while. "So the story comes whole," he said at last, "even as the ring is made whole. But it is a cruel story, Tenar. The little children, that isle, the old man and woman I saw. . . . They scarcely knew human speech."

"I would ask you something."

"Ask."

"I do not wish to go to the Inner Lands, to Havnor. I do not belong there, in the great cities among foreign men. I do not belong to any land. I betrayed my own people. I have no people. And I have done a very evil thing. Put me alone on an island, as the king's children were left, on a lone isle where there are no people, where there is no one. Leave me, and take the ring to Havnor. It is yours, not mine. It has nothing to do with me. Nor have your people. Let me be by myself!"

Slowly, gradually, yet startling her, a light dawned like a small moonrise in the blackness before her; the wizardly light that came at his command. It clung to the end of his staff, which he held upright as he sat facing her in the prow. It lit the bottom of the sail, and the gunwales, and the planking, and his face, with a silvery glow. He was looking straight at her.

"What evil have you done, Tenar?"

"I ordered that three men be shut into a room beneath the Throne, and starved to death. They died of hunger and thirst. They died, and are buried there in the Undertomb. The Tombstones fell on their graves." She stopped.

"Is there more?"

"Manan."

"That death is on my soul."

"No. He died because he loved me, and was faithful. He thought he was protecting me. He held the sword above my neck. When I was little he was kind to me—when I cried—" She stopped again, for the tears rose hard in her, yet she would cry no more. Her hands were clenched on the black folds of her dress. "I was never kind to him," she said. "I will not go to Havnor. I will not go with you. Find some isle where no one comes, and put me there, and leave me. The evil must be paid for. I am *not* free."

The soft light, grayed by sea mist, glimmered between them.

"Listen, Tenar. Heed me. You were the vessel of

evil. The evil is poured out. It is done. It is buried in its own tomb. You were never made for cruelty and darkness; you were made to hold light, as a lamp burning holds and gives its light. I found the lamp unlit; I won't leave it on some desert island like a thing found and cast away. I'll take you to Havnor and say to the princes of Earthsea, 'Look! In the place of darkness I found the light, her spirit. By her an old evil was brought to nothing. By her I was brought out of the grave. By her the broken was made whole, and where there was hatred there will be peace.' "

"I will not," Tenar said in agony. "I cannot. It's not true!"

"And after that," he went on quietly, "I'll take you away from the princes and the rich lords; for it's true that you have no place there. You are too young, and too wise. I'll take you to my own land, to Gont where I was born, to my old master Ogion. He's an old man now, a very great Mage, a man of quiet heart. They call him 'the Silent.' He lives in a small house on the great cliffs of Re Albi, high over the sea. He keeps some goats, and a garden patch. In autumn he goes wandering over the island, alone, in the forests, on the mountainsides, through the valleys of the rivers. I lived there once with him, when I was younger than you are now. I didn't stay long, I hadn't the sense to stay. I went off seeking evil, and sure enough I found it. . . . But you come escaping evil; seeking freedom; seeking silence for a while, until you find your own way. There you will find kindness and silence, Tenar. There the lamp will burn out of the wind awhile. Will you do that?"

The sea mist drifted gray between their faces. The boat lifted lightly on the long waves. Around them was the night and under them the sea.

"I will," she said with a long sigh. And after a long time, "Oh, I wish it were sooner . . . that we could go there now. . . ."

"It won't be long, little one."

"Will you come there, ever?"

"When I can I will come."

The light had died away; it was all dark around them.

They came, after the sunrises and sunsets, the still days and the icy winds of their winter voyage, to the Inmost Sea. They sailed the crowded lanes among great ships, up the Ebavnor Straits and into the bay that lies locked in the heart of Havnor, and across the bay to Havnor Great Port. They saw the white towers, and all the city white and radiant in snow. The roofs of the bridges and the red roofs of the houses were snow-covered, and the rigging of the hundred ships in the harbor glittered with ice in the winter sun. News of their coming had run ahead of them, for *Lookfar's* patched red sail was known in those seas; a great crowd had gathered on the snowy quays, and colored pennants cracked above the people in the bright, cold wind.

Tenar sat in the stern, erect, in her ragged cloak of black. She looked at the ring around her wrist, then at the crowded, many-colored shore and the palaces and the high towers. She lifted up her right hand, and sunlight flashed on the silver of the ring. A cheer went up, faint and joyous on the wind, over the restless water. Ged brought the boat in. A hundred hands reached to catch the rope he flung up to the mooring. He leapt up onto the pier and turned, holding out his hand to her. "Come!" he said smiling, and she rose, and came. Gravely she walked beside him up the white streets of Havnor, holding his hand, like a child coming home.

ABOUT THE AUTHOR

A resident of Portland, Oregon, URSULA K. LE GUIN was born in California, graduated from Radcliffe and earned her master's degree at Columbia University. One of the most distinguished authors of our time and winner of numerous awards, including the National Book Award, the Nebula and the Hugo, she has written many novels and short stories. Among her best known books are *The Left Hand of Darkness, The Dispossessed* and *The Earthsea Trilogy*. Her latest novel is *The Eye of the Heron*.